She'd wanted him to kiss her

Her heart picked up a beat as she remembered the feeling of Ben's arms around her, his mouth poised a hairbreadth away from hers. It had been irresistible, the pull of his lips.

Thank goodness her daughter hadn't seen them kissing. She already saw Ben as a possible father— what would she have thought if she'd seen Julie in his arms?

She had to resist Ben. She had to think of her child. The girl needed a father and stability. If a relationship between Julie and Ben didn't work out, Marisa would be devastated.

And yet... Julie looked back at Ben's house. She could see him through the window. No matter what sense her mind tried to speak, there was no fooling her body. It was no longer deniable: She wanted Ben.

Dear Reader,

February is a month made for romance, and here at Harlequin American Romance we invite *you* to be our Valentine!

Every month, we bring you four reasons to celebrate romance, and beloved author Muriel Jensen has reasons of her own—*Four Reasons for Fatherhood*, to be precise. Join former workaholic Aaron Bradley as he learns about parenthood—and love—from four feisty youngsters and one determined lady in the finale to our exciting miniseries THE DADDY CLUB.

Some men just have a way with women, and our next two heroes are no exception. In Pamela Bauer's *Corporate Cowboy*, when Austin Bennett hits his head and loses his memory, Kacy Judd better watch out—because her formerly arrogant boss is suddenly the most irresistible man in town! And in *Married by Midnight* by Mollie Molay, Maxwell Taylor has more charm than even he suspects—he goes to a wedding one day, and wakes up married the next!

And if you're wondering HOW TO MARRY... *The World's Best Dad*, look no farther than Valerie Taylor's heartwarming tale. Julie Miles may not follow her own advice, but she's got gorgeous Ben Harbison's attention anyway!

We hope you enjoy every romantic minute of our four wonderful stories.

Warm wishes,

Melissa Jeglinski
Associate Senior Editor

HOW TO MARRY...

The World's Best Dad

VALERIE TAYLOR

HARLEQUIN®

TORONTO • NEW YORK • LONDON
AMSTERDAM • PARIS • SYDNEY • HAMBURG
STOCKHOLM • ATHENS • TOKYO • MILAN • MADRID
PRAGUE • WARSAW • BUDAPEST • AUCKLAND

To my father,
Gordon,
who truly was the world's best.
Thanks, Dad.

ISBN 0-373-16816-0

THE WORLD'S BEST DAD

Visit us at www.romance.net

Printed in U.S.A.

ABOUT THE AUTHOR

Valerie Taylor lives in Cincinnati with her husband (the world's second-best daddy) and two young children. In her spare time she reads parenting how-to books and feels inadequate.

Write to her at P.O. Box 42-8825, Cincinnati, OH 45242.

Books by Valerie Taylor

HARLEQUIN AMERICAN ROMANCE
676—THE MOMMY SCHOOL
816—THE WORLD'S BEST DAD

✍ HOW TO BE A DAD:
by Ben Harbison

✔Trust your instincts

✔It's not flying by the seat of your pants—it's spontaneity!

✔Keep your sense of humor—you'll need it!

✍ HOW TO BE A MOM:
by Julie Miles

✔Read all the parenting books

✔Listen to expert advice and make copious notes

✔Have a support team—you'll need it!

Chapter One

"Decision's up to you. Motherhood or your job."

Julie Miles pulled the phone from her ear and looked at it in disgust. Was her boss listening to himself? If the choice was her child or her job, of course, she'd choose Marisa. Ed had kids of his own—why couldn't he understand that?

Then again, he had a spouse to deal with the kids so he could work.

Maybe that's what she needed, a spouse.

She took a deep, calming breath and put the phone back to her ear. "Ed, of course, my job is important to me." For one thing, if she didn't have a job, how would she and Marisa live? "But you know things are a little crazy for me right now. I've been a mom for exactly—" she checked her watch "—forty-three hours and ten minutes. And I've been a home owner for less than twenty-four hours. Cut me a break, will you?"

"I've already given you break after break these past couple weeks," Ed grumbled. "Phillipa

Grange keeps calling, and I know nothing about that stupid program of hers. And you know I've got the brass coming in next week. And here you are, getting on the mommy track. Ridiculous, a twenty-five-year-old with no husband adopting a pre-schooler."

Ed wasn't really a complete jerk, Julie told herself. He was just playing one on the phone.

"Not to mention you leaving me in the lurch with Cincinnati Eagle."

Aha. The real agenda, finally. One of his biggest clients coming in for a presentation later in the week and Ed had no idea how to put the presentation together. He was going to look exceedingly stupid on Friday if something didn't fall his way.

Well, this week, it was his problem. This week, she was a mom. For a moment, she allowed the pure delight of that to distract her from dealing with her boss. She was a mom. She smiled to herself.

"Julie? Are you still there?"

Back to the problem at hand. "Ed, go look in my files under Frequent Flyer Programs. You'll find dozens similar to what Cinci Eagle wants. Make some changes so it looks like you were listening when they told us what they wanted, and give the project to Carla. Believe me, she can do everything I can do."

He grumbled some more, but he let her off the phone. Just in time, too, because the movers were coming up the walk with her box spring. In the rain.

As she watched, they walked through the muddy flower bed—well, weed bed, really—scraped the box spring across the porch railing, and just managed to avoid stepping on the plastic runner they'd spread out to protect her living room carpeting.

Not that she liked the stained mauve carpet, but a coating of mud was not the answer.

Mrs. Malloy, Julie's enormously fat tiger-striped cat, lumbered into the living room carrying the carcass of yet another of the mice she was helpfully hunting in the basement. She deposited it on the living room window seat next to the others. She seemed to be arranging them by size. Julie suppressed a shudder and tried not to think about it.

The burliest of the three movers nodded at her, the wet box spring balanced in his muddy arms. "Where to, lady?"

"Master bedroom, please. Upstairs." They turned and manhandled the box spring upstairs, knocking hard into a railing as they negotiated the turn in the stairs. Julie reached over to check it. Yep, loose. Of course, it had probably been loose before. Everything in the house was either loose or painted shut. Her new home was a handyman's special.

Unfortunately, Julie barely knew which was the business end of a screwdriver. She made a note to herself to find a book on home repairs.

"Julie? Where's my stuff?" Marisa—the reason for all of this, for everything Julie had done in the past month—hesitated slightly at the top of the stairs before starting down, as if she weren't sure what she was doing was okay. The five-year-old had been bounced from foster home to her mother and back again for the past four and a half years. But now she finally had a forever family: Julie.

Marisa blushed. "I mean, *Mom*." She looked down, and Julie felt the little girl's embarrassment. "Sorry, I forgot," she said on the barest whisper.

Julie squatted next to her. "Marisa, it's okay if you forget. It's hard to remember at first. I keep forgetting, too. Then I remember—I have a daughter!" She smiled in delight and Marisa smiled back. Julie pulled her into a big hug. The too-skinny little body stiffened for a moment, then relaxed. Marisa wasn't quite ready to hug back, but in the days since the adoption papers had been signed, she'd been getting more comfortable. Julie knew Marisa still didn't quite believe it was for real, but the hope, heartbreaking in its fragility, was always in her eyes.

Marisa pulled away slightly, looking over Julie's shoulder into the living room, and Julie let her go. Her eyes widened, and her lips drew back in distaste. "Mom! What's *that*?"

Julie turned around. Mrs. Malloy's mice, that's what that was. "Oh, that's just a mess I'm getting ready to clean up. Don't look, honey." She hurried into the kitchen to find some paper towels and an empty grocery sack.

When she returned, Marisa was leaning over the window seat. "Gross!"

Julie turned her away from the sight. "Don't worry, honey, I'm going to take care of it."

"Mary wouldn't take care of it. Mary would make George take care of it." Mary and George had been Marisa's most recent foster parents. "Mary says daddies do that."

"Well, in this house, I do that." Brave words, but the familiar anxiety hit Julie in the pit of her stomach anyway. It seemed as if every time she turned around there was yet another message that kids needed both a mother and a father.

When Marisa didn't appear to be convinced by Julie's words, Julie patted her on the shoulder reassuringly. "Honey, if daddies can do it, so can mommies." That was what Julie kept telling herself, anyway. It didn't stop her stomach from rebelling as she picked up the dead mice and dropped them into the sack.

After Julie had disposed of the bodies, Marisa apparently remembered her original errand. "Mom, my stuff isn't here!" She looked up into Julie's eyes anxiously. Her "stuff"—the pitifully little amount that there was—was in two cardboard boxes in Julie's car.

"That's okay, I know where it is. It's in my car, safe and dry."

Marisa screwed her face into a doubtful frown.

Julie smiled, resigned to getting wet. "Okay,

let's go get it." She stood and took Marisa's hand, and they walked out onto the porch. "Ready?" Marisa nodded. "Okay, let's go!" Still holding hands, they ran out into the downpour and across the front yard to the car.

Julie yanked open the hatchback of her elderly navy-blue Saab and dragged out a cardboard carton. "Here, you take this one, I'll get the big one." She grabbed the other carton and balanced it on her hip while she jerked the hatchback shut. The two of them hurried back through the rain to the porch, laughing as they got drenched.

They carried the boxes upstairs to Marisa's room. Marisa dived into the first to check her most treasured possessions, her battered, much-read books. Julie smiled at her intensity. It was one of the things she'd loved first about Marisa. For a moment, before getting back to work, Julie simply watched and enjoyed her daughter.

Wringing water from her brown hair, Julie trotted back down the stairs and into the living room just as her friend Carla Hartshorn came through the front door, her own short blond curls dripping. The two of them probably looked worse than Mrs. Malloy's mice.

Julie raised her eyebrows. "Ed let you leave? I just got off the phone with him, and he was panicking."

Carla grinned. "I'm on my lunch hour."

"At four in the afternoon?"

"I didn't get lunch earlier, due to him freaking out. Good idea of yours, having him go through an old presentation and mark it up. That'll keep him busy all night."

"Yeah, but it'll leave you with the cleanup tomorrow."

Carla shrugged her dainty shoulders. "I know what you wanted for Cinci Eagle, so it shouldn't be a problem. Now, what can I do to help?"

Julie gave her a grateful look. "Bless you, my child. You can call the plumber and find out why he still isn't here even though we had a nine-o'clock appointment and every time I call they say we're the next stop. And you can call Cincinnati Power & Light and find out why we still don't have electricity even though they were supposed to turn it on this morning." She handed Carla her cell phone and the list of calls she'd made. "And Cincinnati Telephone, too, while you're at it, to find out why the phone hasn't been turned on. All these cell calls are going to break me."

Carla clicked the phone. "No, they won't."

Julie shot her a questioning glance.

Carla held up the phone. "Battery's dead."

Wonderful.

BEN HARBISON TURNED from his four-year-old son in the bathtub to grab the portable phone on the sink behind him. "Hello?"

"Ben?"

He sighed to himself. Maggie. A nice woman, a wonderful grandmother, but she'd been trying to run his life and Joe's ever since Rose died two years ago. "Hi, Maggie. What's up?"

"Ben, I'm concerned about Joey."

No surprise. Maggie was always concerned about Joey. Ben glanced at his son. "Just a minute, Maggie." He covered the mouthpiece for a moment. "No splashing, understand?"

Joe frowned. "Cats don't splash. Cats don't like water."

A cat. Well, a cat was better than a rabbit, which Joe had been for three carrot-filled days last month. Ben had worried the kid would turn orange.

"Excellent!" Ben handed his son the washcloth. "You can give yourself a nice cat-bath with this cat-tongue."

Ben stepped out into the hall so Joe wouldn't hear the conversation. Lately, his conversations with Maggie were never good and were getting worse, instead of better. Joe didn't need to hear an argument between the two most important people in his world. "Okay, I'm back. Now, what about Joe?"

"I don't like that day-care center he goes to."

Ben bit his tongue and paced down the hall to keep from replying sharply. "Maggie, it's a preschool. And he's very happy there, and it's only ten minutes from the job site."

She hesitated a moment. "I think he'd be better off here with me."

Why were they wasting time on this argument again? Ben tried to control his irritation. Pacing back down the hall and into his bedroom, he gave her the same answer he'd given her last time she'd suggested she watch Joe during the day. "That's impossible. You're an hour away, and I can't see how spending two hours each day in the car is good for Joe."

Much less the four hours Ben would spend driving Joe back and forth. But he knew better than to bring up that. "Maggie, we've been through this before, several times—"

She broke in, hurrying to get the words said. "I mean, during the week. He could stay here with me."

He almost laughed. "Stay with you? You mean overnight?"

Her voice took on new resolution. "I think we should talk about Joey living here with me during the week. He could go to preschool here, a couple mornings a week instead of all day every day." Maggie started to talk faster. "You could come get him on Friday nights, and bring him back Sunday nights. Or even Monday mornings. That way you'd only have to take time out of your workday once each week."

Ben was speechless.

"Don't you think that's a much better idea than

driving back and forth?'' Her voice turned whee-
dling. ''And think how much more freedom you'd
have during the week.''

He gritted his teeth. She'd always thought that
was the real issue with Ben. His own convenience.
For a moment, resentment flared. Did she really
think he liked having Joe in preschool nine hours a
day? Carefully he tamped down on his emotions
before he lost his temper.

She continued. ''And this way he wouldn't have
to spend such a long time in day care each day.
And I don't mind a bit—you know how Joey and
I get along.''

''Joe.''

''Pardon?''

''Joe. He hates being called Joey.'' Ben took a
breath. ''Maggie, you can't possibly have thought
this idea would fly with me. I appreciate your offer,
but of course I want Joe here with me.''

He could almost hear her stiffening. ''Perhaps
what you want and what is best for Joey are two
different things.''

There it was. That's what it always came down
to. Ben's selfishness. He felt guilty and anxious
enough about Joe's preschool schedule. He didn't
need Maggie adding to it with advice and suggestions that tore him up inside.

''I'm his father. I know what's best for him.'' He
took a breath to calm himself and made a conscious
effort to lower the tone of his voice. ''Maggie, you

know I've always loved and respected you. I understand you think Joe needs something different than I'm giving him. I respect your opinion, but I think you're wrong. I understand you're saying these things out of love for Joe. But I can't put this any other way—back off."

She gasped, probably at the dead-serious tone of his voice as much as the words themselves, and he felt another stab of guilt for hurting her. Then she gave an offended huff. "I am the child's grandparent. The only living representative of his mother's family. I have a responsibility to make sure he is being cared for properly."

"Then I can assure you, Joe is being very well cared for. Unless you think I'm incapable of doing a good job, you're just going to have to accept that." He took another deep breath and tried a warmer tone. "Look, I know you only want what's best for Joe. That's the same thing I want. Trust me. You must know I'm doing my level best here. Do you believe that?" He paused, waiting for her response.

"Of course, Ben." Her voice sounded muffled, flat.

"And if you believe I'm doing my best, can't you give me enough credit to believe my best is good enough?" He hated the hint of pleading he heard in his own voice, the implication that he didn't believe it himself.

She sighed, sounding resigned for now. "I believe you believe it."

He shook his head. There was no winning. "Maggie, listen, I have to go. Joe's in the tub, and it's way too quiet in there." At her disapproving gasp, he closed his eyes in disgust at his own stupidity. Why had he told her Joe was unsupervised in the tub?

He knew he'd never manage to keep his tongue through one more lecture on parenting practices. "Look, Maggie, we'll talk more later." He hung up before she could protest.

He hadn't heard the end of it, but at least it was the end for tonight. Maybe next time he talked to her he'd have more patience.

He headed back toward the bathroom, deliberately willing himself to calm down before he walked in on his son. Joe didn't deserve the remnants of Ben's irritation with Maggie.

He looked at his watch. Only four o'clock, but after a full day on the site and only a half hour with his son, he was beat. Maybe he could get Joe down to bed early tonight.

He'd get Joe bathed and fed and played with and read to and put to bed and put to bed again and put to bed sternly and put to bed with dire threats. Then Ben could start mentally recharging himself for the next day. When had he gotten so old?

He stepped into the bathroom.

No Joe.

JULIE STOOD STARING at the dead phone stupidly.

In the open doorway, one of the movers grunted as all three tried to maneuver her wet living room couch through the opening.

Mrs. Malloy walked past her and into the living room with yet another body for her collection.

Julie felt like throwing the dead cell phone on the floor and stomping on it. With an effort, she controlled herself. She was a mom now, she had to be mature. All the parenting books emphasized the importance of the role model she played for her daughter. Especially since she was the female parent. Especially since she was the only parent. She had to be practically perfect. The knowledge settled like a familiar weight on her shoulders.

She took a deep breath to calm herself. It didn't really work but she did manage to keep from doing violence to the phone.

She peered out the dining room window at the house next door. Maybe the neighbor had a cordless. Or even a phone with a long cord. There was only a slim strip of driveway between the two houses—the two identical tiny bungalows had obviously been shoehorned in on what had originally been a single lot long after the rest of the neighborhood had already been built.

Fine, she'd go meet her new neighbor.

She called up the stairs. "Marisa? I'm going next door for a minute. Carla's here."

"Take me with you!" Marisa ran from her bedroom into the small hall at the top of the stairs. Her nervous glance shot to Carla and back to Julie. Carla gave Marisa an encouraging smile, but Marisa was having none of it. It wasn't that she didn't like Carla. She just couldn't seem to let Julie out of her sight.

Julie looked out the door as the movers tried again with the couch. "But it's raining, honey."

Marisa ran down the stairs. "That's okay."

Julie shrugged at Carla. "Okay, we'll both get wet."

Carla was watching Marisa. "Can I come, too?"

Marisa nodded, and Carla mouthed "progress" at Julie.

Julie laughed. "I think you're both nuts. But, okay, we'll all three get wet."

The movers set the couch down half in, half out of the living room door. "Lady, I think this door is going to have to come off."

Of course it was. Julie gave them a resigned nod.

Carla looked at her with a wide-eyed gaze. "For free? Boy, are you lucky! Is this place ever going to be nice and aired out! No better smell than a nice spring rain, I always say."

Julie gave a helpless laugh. What would she do without Carla? Feeling quite lucky, indeed, Julie led Carla and Marisa out the back door.

It was dim under the overhang of the awning, the early March sun already setting behind the rain clouds.

"Should we just run over to their back door? It's closer." Carla nodded across the yard.

"Yeah, but I hate to introduce myself that way. Let's go around to the front like civilized people. It's not much farther, and we're going to be wet anyway."

She held out her hand to Marisa, but before the three of them could dash out into the drizzle, the back door of the neighboring house swung open, and a naked child streaked across the two small backyards to Julie's sandbox.

Into which he promptly peed.

Chapter Two

"Oh, my," Carla said.

Next door, the back door swung open again, and out ran a tallish man with short dark hair wearing jeans and pulling a faded T-shirt over his head.

"Oh, *my*," Carla said.

The man stopped and scanned the yards. "Joe?" His gaze lit on the boy. "Joe! No!"

He sprinted across the yard and grabbed the child, lifting him off the ground and onto his hip. He shook his head. "Joe! What in the world are you doing?"

"I'm a cat! I need to use the litter box!" The boy struggled within the man's bare arms. The man had no trouble maintaining his grasp, but the muscles in his shoulders shifted with the child's movements, straining just enough to bring them into sharper focus. The misting rain added a sheen to his tan, and Julie found herself staring.

He looked up at that moment, to where Julie stood under the tattered awning. She blushed, though she doubted he could have noticed more than that she was watching him with the struggling child, who by now was shrieking in frustrated protest.

"Sorry, I didn't see you there." He pulled the shirt back over his head and dropped it over that of the child, walked the few steps from the sandbox and ducked under the awning. He set the boy down, but he kept a firm grasp on the child's wrist. "My son. He's a cat, you know. Last week he was a turtle. Apparently turtles can use toilets." He looked from her to Carla to Marisa, who was staring at Joe with her mouth open, and gave Julie an amused grin. "Ben Harbison."

"Julie Miles." She held out her hand.

He took it, enveloping it in his own large one. His palm felt warm and slightly rough on hers, a little damp from the rain, and she was suddenly very aware of his nearness, as if his presence was somehow more profound than normal.

His eyes met her own, and she felt a jolt of recognition, two adults sharing the knowledge that each found the other attractive. She bit back a smile. "And this is my daughter, Marisa." She and Marisa grinned at each other, enjoying the word.

He leaned down to offer his hand to Marisa, who transferred her rapt attention from Joe to Ben. She smiled in delight. "Are you a daddy?"

Julie suppressed a sigh of anxiety. Clearing her

throat, she nodded at Carla. "And, ah, this is my friend, Carla Hartshorn."

Carla grinned at him, all teeth, and Julie stiffened in anticipation of something embarrassing. Carla didn't disappoint. "So, you and your wife been in this neighborhood very long?"

Julie fought the urge to close her eyes in mortification. Leave it to Carla to go straight for the marital status.

His smile twitched as he reached for Carla's hand, his expression acute but good-natured. Julie could see in his face that he understood the question completely, and when he switched his glance to her, she almost laughed at the awareness she saw there. She smiled, sharing the joke with him.

"We've been here five years, and we'll probably be here forever. We like the neighborhood. But it's just me and Joe." The child at his side tugged on his arm, and he gave Julie a wry smile. "Which reminds me. The one with no clothes is Joe, the terror of the neighborhood. I'll replace the sand in your sandbox and clean it tomorrow."

He pulled his son around to face him and leaned over to look into the child's eyes. "Apologize to Ms. Miles, and promise her you won't do that again."

"But I'm a cat!" Indignant exasperation.

His father took him by the chin. "Then you better learn to be a cat with manners, because cats without them end up staying in the house a lot.

Apologize.'' He released both chin and wrist and straightened, expectant.

Joe eyed Julie, then looked at the ground. ''Sorry.''

''And?'' His father's tone was insistent. He wasn't letting his son off that easy.

''And I won't do it anymore.'' But as he said it, Joe cast a calculating gaze toward the sandbox, as if trying to come up with some loophole.

Julie didn't quite know what to say. She didn't remember Marisa ever misbehaving like this, or shrieking at anyone, not in the four years she'd known her. Plus Julie was a little uncomfortable with the fact she was talking to an almost naked person, even if he was just a little boy. ''Well, that's okay, Joe. I'm pleased to meet you, and thank you for not…um, using the sandbox that way anymore.''

She cleared her throat and looked again at Ben. ''Actually, I was just coming over to ask if I could borrow a phone.'' She held up her dead cell phone. ''Murphy's Law.''

He nodded. ''Be my guest. In fact, it's a portable. Joe and I'll go get it for you. No use you getting wet, too.''

Marisa, who'd been staring at Joe again, said, ''Cats don't like rain.''

Joe stopped struggling for a moment. Julie almost laughed at the expression on his face as he considered that pronouncement.

Ben hoisted Joe back up onto his hip. ''I better take advantage of the temporary lull in motion while he works that one out. Just give me a couple minutes to get something warm on him, and we'll be right back over.''

Julie thanked him, but he waved her off. ''That's what neighbors are for. Go back inside, get out of the weather.''

Throwing the small boy over his bare shoulder, he headed toward their house. Joe bounced up and down, hooting with glee as they crossed the yard in the drizzle.

Marisa went to investigate the sandbox. Julie bit back a smile as the little girl peered over the edge, then turned to look at the neighbor's house, her face full of curiosity.

Carla breathed out. ''Man, you have all the luck, moving in next door to that.''

''What, a small boy who'll pee in my sandbox? Yup, I've got the luck of the Irish, all right.''

Carla laughed. ''The father, silly. He's quite the specimen. I wonder if he wanders around without his shirt all the time? I wonder if that's all natural, or if he works out? Want me to find out for you?'' She peered over at the darkened windows of the house next door, as if trying for a peek inside. ''And he's going to be living there for a while. Did you notice I found that out for you?''

Julie gave her a wry look. ''I noticed. And that

he's single, too. And, no, please don't find out anything else.''

"Subtlety was never my strong suit." Carla grinned. "So shoot me."

"He is pretty cute, isn't he?" Julie pretended to peer at the windows, too. "You know, if I trimmed that hedge a bit, I bet we could sit on the patio at night and, well, see what's what."

"Voyeurs R Us." Carla kept her face straight. "I like it. We could probably sell tickets."

They both jumped when a light appeared in one of the windows. When Ben followed his son into what was obviously the child's bedroom, Julie gave a guilty laugh. "Guess I don't need to trim the hedges after all." She called Marisa, and they turned to go into the house.

The big mover was poking his head into the kitchen when Julie stepped in from the patio. "Oh, there you are, lady. Come here, I think you better look at this."

Julie's heart sank as she followed him upstairs, trailed by Marisa. What now?

Upstairs, in the bedroom that was supposed to be Julie's, the mover opened the closet door. The floor was covered with water, which had splashed onto the walls.

Julie looked up at the ceiling of the closet at a large, dark stain. As they watched, a drop of water formed and fell to puddle on the floor, splashing the walls.

Marisa looked at the wet spot, then up at Julie. "If we had a daddy, I bet he could fix it."

BEN KNELT ON THE FLOOR in front of Joe's bed and hustled the now-shivering child into a sweatshirt and sweatpants. Joe's feet were clammy as he slid socks over them. "Weren't you cold out there?"

"N-no!" Joe shook his head, stubborn. "Cats aren't cold outside. Cats are cold inside, though."

Ben bit back a laugh and gathered the child into his arms, rubbing him to warm him. He held him close for a moment, enjoying the feel of the small body in his arms. How much longer would Joe let his father cuddle him close? Ben felt a pang of yearning, part of him wishing he could keep Joe four years old forever. Nuzzling his neck and making snarfing noises, Ben carried Joe to the living room, grabbing the portable phone on his way out the front door.

The two of them stepped under the front porch overhang at the new neighbors'. The front door was off the hinges, so Ben called in through the open doorway, "Telephone man."

Julie came around the corner, her red and white sweater setting off the flush of her face—not to mention hugging her curves. The faded jeans didn't say anything bad about her, either. She smiled at him, her lips parting in a fascinating way. The little girl, Marisa, followed right behind her, almost clinging to her side.

He held up the phone. "It should be all charged up, and at this distance you shouldn't have any trouble. But if you do, I can bring over the charger."

She shook her head. "Won't do any good. No electricity."

Marisa tugged on Julie's arm. "It's 'cause we don't have a daddy. A daddy could turn the lights on."

Ben watched Julie bite her lip and sympathized. Joe was almost as good as Maggie at making Ben aware of all that he was not. He smiled at Marisa. "I thought you people just liked having the lights out."

Marisa laughed, and as he watched, Julie relaxed ever so slightly. "It was supposed to be turned on, but they still haven't gotten to it. That was one of the things we needed the phone for." She glanced over her shoulder as Carla walked into the room from the kitchen. "I was going to sic Carla on them."

"Grrr," said Carla.

He turned the handset over and started pushing buttons. "Here, let me try."

"I'm sure Carla can handle it."

Carla said, "Oh, let him try. Men love fixing problems. Makes them feel useful." She grinned at Ben.

He finished dialing, then listened while it rang.

"Alberta Owen, please." He waited a moment while the call was transferred.

Her line clicked on. "Alberta."

"Alberta. Baby. Sweetheart." He smiled, waiting for it.

"*Ben!* Ben Harbison, you better not be sweet-talking me for help at four fifty-five at night. I'm late for the door."

"Guilty."

"Rascal. What is it?"

"My new neighbor. She was supposed to have her power turned on, but it hasn't happened. She's moving into a dark house with her little girl."

"Address?"

"Fifteen sixty-five Glenbeck."

"Oh, *right* next door, hmm? And is she pretty, this new neighbor?"

His eyes shot to Julie, who was watching him. "Uh, yes."

"And will this make you the hero?"

He coughed. "Well, it wouldn't hurt any."

"Mmm-hmm. So Alberta gets to play Cupid, does she? Let me see…" He heard her fingers on her keyboard. "Mmm-hmm, should have gone on today. I can take care of it from here." Another few keystrokes. "Okay, ready?"

"Ready."

The living room's overhead light came on.

Carla gasped.

Marisa clapped, and when Joe said, "My daddy

can do anything,'' she turned to Ben, her eyes shining.

Ben grinned and looked at Julie. She was staring at him in astonishment, her mouth slightly open. He said into the mouthpiece, "Thank you, Alberta."

"Mmm-hmm. Invite me to the wedding, hear?" She clicked off.

He pressed the off button on the phone and held it out to Julie. She stared at it for a moment, then at him. For a moment, her deep blue eyes on his, he was sure he'd blown it. Too sure of himself, as usual. He toned down his grin for a moment.

Finally she smiled back at him. "Do you know anyone at Cincinnati Water? They keep saying they've turned the water on, but there's no water."

Ben swallowed. "Er…did you check the main valve to the house?"

Carla snorted.

Julie narrowed her eyes at her friend in exaggerated irritation. "The main valve? No one said anything about a main valve."

Ben tried not to smile. "I'm sure very few people know about it. It's practically a secret."

She turned her mock displeasure on him. "Just go get a wrench or something, okay?"

"Right. C'mon, Joe." He made his escape.

Ben found his tool belt and strapped it on, then walked around Julie's house until he found the water shutoff valve. Yep, it was off. He adjusted the fitting, then walked back into her house, Joe at his heels. "Try it now," he said.

Julie walked into the bathroom under the stairs, and he heard the water running. She came back out. "It's brown, but at least it's running."

Joe, apparently realizing he was trailing around after a bunch of adults doing boring stuff, turned to Marisa. "Do you like swings?"

Marisa nodded and smiled shyly at him.

"Want to go swing?"

Marisa nodded, and the little boy grabbed her hand and tugged at her. She turned to Julie.

Julie glanced through the open doorway. "Well, it's starting to get a little dark...." She looked at Marisa. "But at least it's stopped raining. Go ahead, honey."

The two children ran off, and Ben followed Julie into the kitchen. She watched as they ran through the backyard to Ben's house. She turned to him, frowning slightly. "They'll be okay, won't they?"

Ben nodded. What could happen to them? "They're just out in the backyard. It's probably been a pretty boring day for her, with moving and all."

She bit her lip. "I guess we can see them from here. Well, then, now that I have water—" Carla smirked, and Julie ignored her "—I guess I'll start unpacking boxes." She opened one of the cupboards and coughed as dust flew out.

He glanced over her shoulder into the cupboard,

which was thick with dust. "Why don't you let me wipe out those cupboards for you before you put stuff away?"

She smiled. "You're hired."

Carla grabbed her purse off the kitchen counter. "Sounds too much like work to me. I'm off for those curtain rods. Back in a flash." She waved goodbye on her way out, and Ben heard her tell the movers the door better be back on its hinges when she returned. So she'd be back. He'd better work fast.

Julie smiled at him. "Thanks for the offer of help. You really don't have to stay."

Ben shook his head. "I don't mind at all. A little adult company is always welcome." And now that they were alone, he wasn't going to waste the opportunity. He grabbed a bunch of paper towels from a roll and wet them at the sink. "And I can see you have your hands full. I guess all single parents do."

She turned slightly away from him, leaning over to open a box. "It's just all so new, I guess."

He tried not to leer at her backside, with limited success. It was a very nice backside. What the hell, she couldn't see him. He jerked his gaze from her jeans as she turned around. He had to think a minute before he could remember what she'd just said. "Ah, what, being a single parent?"

She nodded. "I just adopted Marisa two days ago."

"Brave woman, walking into single parenting with your eyes open."

She laughed. "I don't know how open they were." She turned half away, started rinsing a pile of plates one by one, stacking them on the counter, her arms graceful, in and out of the water. "I was her *guardian ad litem* for four years. She's been in foster care, and when she had to be moved to a new foster home, I just couldn't stand to see her have to start all over again."

"So you decided to adopt her? Just like that?"

"More or less." She made a wry face, and he guessed it had been a little more complicated than that. She dried the stack of plates and set them into the cupboard above the dishwasher.

"Do you get a lot of people telling you how much they admire you?"

She laughed. "Yes. And so far I've felt like I'm doing a totally unadmirable job."

"Oh, that never ends. It's always going to be harder when you're going it alone. You don't have anyone to bounce your thoughts off." He shook his head. "Or if you do, sometimes they end up making you feel worse." She turned to him, concern clear on her face, and he gave her a wry grin. "I'm guessing I'm not making you feel any better, here."

She laughed at that. "Not at all. But next time you need to bounce some thoughts off someone, come bounce them off me. I'll try not to make you feel worse." She smiled, that fascinating curve of slightly parted lips. What was it about her smile? If he didn't watch out, he could lose himself in it.

She crossed to the stack of unopened boxes again, struggling for a moment opening one. He pulled his penknife out of his pocket and squatted beside her, his knees brushing hers lightly. She moved out of his way, and he wished she hadn't.

For the next half hour, while the movers put the door back on its hinges and cleaned up after themselves, he and Julie worked together, she unpacking boxes, rinsing dishes and pans, and putting them away; he wiping cupboards and trying not to obviously watch her stretching and bending and doing other fascinating things.

Just as Julie was finishing stacking pots in the cupboard under the stove, Carla returned, her arms sprouting curtain rods, and Marisa came in from the backyard with Joe. "Julie...Mom, I mean. I'm hungry."

"Me, too, Dad." Big surprise. The kid had a hollow leg.

Julie looked as if all she wanted to do was collapse on the couch, but she grinned at Marisa. "I hope you're willing to have peanut butter for dinner, then, because I am not up to cooking."

"How about we call for pizza?" Ben looked around for the phone. "My treat—in honor of Marisa's first day in her new house." He gave Marisa a smile, and she rewarded him with a bright one of her own. Nice kid, that one. "You do like pizza, right?"

Marisa nodded, her eyes wide. "I love pizza."

"Yea, pizza!" Joe jumped up and down. "Spicy Tomato, Daddy!" He turned to Marisa. "That's the best one. But LaMama's is good, too. We get pizza all the time, so we know the best ones."

"Well, not all the time," Ben said.

"Yeah, we have macaroni and cheese sometimes, too." Joe pursed his lips. "I like Power Rangers macaroni and cheese better than Rugrats, Daddy." He turned back to Marisa. "But if we get Spicy Tomato, we have to eat all of it, because Spicy Tomato isn't as good at breakfast. LaMama's is, though, huh, Daddy?"

Ben grinned, a little weakly. Carla said, "That's what you get for teaching kids to talk."

As the five of them were eating the pizza, Ben picked up a flier that had been delivered with it. Noted Parenting Expert Maynard Frader To Speak.

That Frader idiot again. Maggie was forever clipping his column and bringing it with her when she visited. He tossed the flier on the table.

Julie picked it up. She pursed her lips. "This is what I need."

"That windbag! What about him?"

Julie laughed. "Maybe you should at least hear what he has to say before you call him a windbag."

"I've read his column. The man has no idea of the real challenges facing parents."

"He's supposed to be an expert."

Some expert. "How can he be an expert when he has no kids of his own?"

"He has a Ph.D., that's how."

Carla was watching them, her avid gaze switching from one to the other as if she were watching a Ping-Pong match.

Ben bit his tongue. Better to say nothing than to get himself in trouble.

Julie eyed him suspiciously, as if she knew what he was thinking. "You think you know all the answers, don't you?"

He shrugged. "Of course not. I just know what's best for my kid."

"And you don't think you could improve things?"

"Not by listening to a bunch of advice from someone who probably doesn't know any more than I do."

Julie frowned at the flier. "But how could it hurt?"

"It could confuse you, that's how it could hurt." He took a bite of pizza to give himself a minute to think. "He says one thing, someone else says something else. Who's right? You just have to trust your instincts."

"That's your whole parenting plan? Trust your instincts?"

He shrugged. "It's worked so far."

She eyed him, looking unconvinced. She had great eyes, a great color of blue. Even when they were all narrowed up like that. He took another bite of pizza and grinned at her, and an answering smile crept over her lips. She knew he was enjoying the view and she didn't seem to mind a bit.

Now, *this* was an interesting woman.

AFTER BEN AND JOE LEFT for the night, Julie said to Marisa, "Bedtime."

"What about my bath?"

"Oh, right. Bath time, I mean." Another first. Was there any special trick to bathing a five-year-old? She looked at Carla.

"You're on your own, girlfriend. It's the kind of thing you can only learn by doing." Carla lay back on the couch. "Besides, I'm exhausted from my exertions."

Julie found the pile of boxes marked "Books" and pulled the largest one open. *Every Parent's Guide To Doing The Right Thing* was on top. Julie had been reading it up until the movers arrived at her old apartment.

She paged through the index while she led Marisa upstairs, leaving Carla on the couch with a glass of wine and the *Cincinnati Enquirer*.

Bathing, page 42.

Remember that a child's skin is very delicate. What seems like a reasonable temperature to an adult can feel burning hot to a young child.... Remember never to leave a baby or young child alone in a bathtub. Young children can drown in even a few inches of water and in less time than it takes to answer the phone....

How young was too young, Julie wondered. Could a five-year-old really drown in a bathtub?

She ran the water. Marisa stepped in and Julie hovered over the tub, one hand steady on Marisa's arm in case she slipped. Marisa sat down and looked up at her expectantly. "Do we got bubbles?"

"Bubbles." How could she make bubbles? Shampoo, maybe? Julie opened the nearest box and pushed things around inside, looking for the green bottle. She poured some shampoo into the stream of water. It bubbled beautifully, and Marisa clapped. "Bubbles!" She splashed, then looked up at Julie anxiously.

"Don't worry, honey, just try to keep it in the tub."

She washed the little girl's long dark hair, then watched her splash a bit. She'd have to get some bath toys.

"All ready?"

Marisa nodded, and Julie helped her out of the tub and into a towel. She dried her off, rubbing the too-thin little legs and arms gently, hugging her through the towel as she dried off her back. "Oh, Marisa, I'm so glad you came to live with me. I'm so glad I'm your mom now."

Marisa stiffened. Then, almost convulsively, her arms went around Julie and hugged her back. Julie almost cried.

She helped Marisa into her pajamas and made up her bed for her. "Shall we read a story? Which one do you want to read?"

Marisa knelt by the small pile of well-worn books—Julie added a bookcase to her list of things to buy—and pulled out an especially tattered one. *Sharing Danny's Dad.* The story of a little boy who one day shared his best friend's dad while his own father was away at work. The Trocens, Marisa's foster family before Mary and George, had given it to her last year for Christmas. She'd wanted it read to her almost daily.

As Julie was tucking Marisa in, she could tell the little girl had something on her mind. "What's up, honey?"

"Mom, can I share Joe's dad?"

Julie froze her face, trying to keep from showing any dismay. "Well, I'm sure you can be good friends with Ben."

"But I can't share him?"

Julie sighed silently. "I guess you can share him a little, sometimes."

She kissed Marisa good-night and walked back

downstairs. She sat down next to Carla on the couch, poured herself a glass of wine and propped her feet on the battered coffee table. "Marisa wants a dad."

Carla shrugged. "Everyone wants a dad. I want a dad."

"I know. But Marisa really needs a father. More than most kids do. It's all she talks about. It's as if getting a mother gave her hope that she could actually get both." Tears stung Julie's eyes and she wiped them away.

Carla watched her, sympathy in her eyes. "So get her a dad."

Julie snorted. "As if it were that easy."

Carla leaned back and put her feet on the coffee table, too. "What's so difficult about it? You weren't planning on staying single forever, were you?"

"Well, no. But things are different now. For one thing, he has to be a really great dad."

Shrugging, Carla said, "Then find one of those."

"How do you find 'one of those'?"

Carla smirked at her. "Well, it would help if you were actually dating someone."

"Thanks so much."

"My pleasure."

Julie thought for a moment. "Okay, so I date. How do I recognize a great dad?"

"I think it's just something you have to take a chance on." Carla thought for a moment. "Don't you think most well-intentioned people probably end up being pretty good parents?''

Probably true, for most kids. But Marisa wasn't most kids. ''But is it enough to be a pretty good parent? Marisa needs a *great* parent.''

''She's got you. That's one great parent.''

Julie shook her head. ''But I know nothing.'' Every new day proved that to her in alarming ways. She felt as if she were treading on eggshells with Marisa, trying not to make some huge permanent mistake.

''You know what you *want* to be, as a parent. Just find a guy who wants the same.''

It sounded simple, but Julie knew better. ''No, he needs to be better than me. He needs to be enough to make up for me. To make up for my shortcomings. Someone who knows what he's doing. I need to find someone who can be a great dad.''

Carla laughed. ''So falling in love doesn't enter into it?''

Julie smiled at her friend, sheepish. ''Of course, I have to love him, too. But if it's just as easy to fall in love with a rich man as a poor one, then it ought to be just as easy to fall in love with a good father as a bad one.'' She collapsed against the cushions, frustrated. ''Which brings us right back to figuring out which ones are the good ones. And then dating them.''

Carla leaned forward. ''And falling in love.''

Julie gave her a frown of mock exasperation. "Of course, and falling in love. Sometimes you tend to harp, were you aware of that?" It was a plan, though. It just might work. "If I only date men who would be good fathers, then that's the only kind of guy I'll be able to fall in love with."

"What, you figure once you're ready to fall in love, it'll happen with whoever is close by?" Carla hooted. "Somehow I don't think that's how it works."

"Well, it'll at least be more likely that way."

"Okay, so you stay away from known pedophiles."

Julie laughed. "It's more than that. I want to find a man who will be *good* for Marisa, not just one who won't be bad for her."

Carla thought for a moment. "You know, I read an article once about where to find single men." She had the grace to blush at Julie's raised eyebrow. "Well, there was nothing else to read at the gynecologist's except *Cosmo* and a pamphlet on breast self-exams. Anyway, it said you look for single men in the places single men are. Like, you sign up for group golf lessons because the class is likely to be filled with men. So why don't you look for good fathers in the places they hang out?"

Julie shot her a look. "You know, that is a very good idea."

"I know. I'm full of good ideas. I always tell you that and you never listen." Carla leaned back, chewing on her lip. "Where does someone who would be a good father hang out?"

"I'll tell you where." Julie got up and walked into the kitchen. She picked up the flier she'd read earlier and brought it back to Carla. "Here's where."

Carla looked at it. "At parenting workshops? Wouldn't those be full of guys who think they aren't very good parents and need help?"

Julie brushed that aside. "Not the people attending. The guy giving the lecture."

Carla squinted at the picture, then read the caption. "'Maynard Frader, Ph.D., is a noted child psychologist and author of several books on parenting.'" She shook her head. "I dunno. He looks kind of geeky to me."

Julie snatched the paper back and looked at the picture. "That's not geeky." Or at least, not very geeky. "That's warm and kindly. He has his chin propped on his hands, like he's really listening to someone."

Balancing her glass, Carla leaned over to look at the picture again. "Well, at least he doesn't have a wedding ring on. But he's no Fabio."

"How can you even tell from that little picture? Besides, Fabio isn't even a dad." She sat back down and Carla plopped onto the couch next to her. "Don't you see? That's it. All I have to do is look for parenting experts. Or child-raising experts." It was so simple, really. Almost elegant. "Where do you find the world's best parents? You look for those who do it for a living.''

''Well,'' Carla said doubtfully. ''I suppose you could go hear him speak, maybe chat him up afterward if he doesn't seem like a complete dork.''

''Or even if he does, a second chance couldn't hurt.''

''So, fine, that's one. What if you hate him? We better have some backups.'' Carla reached into her purse and pulled out a notepad. She opened it to a fresh page and headlined it ''The World's Best Dad,'' then added a second headline, ''Candidates.''

Under that, she wrote, ''Maynard Frader, Ph.D. Noted child psychologist. Author of parenting books. Kind of a dork.''

She looked up at Julie, pen poised over the page. ''Now we're cooking with gas. Where else can you look?''

''Hmm, let me think.'' Marisa's social worker had sent Julie a schedule of parenting classes in anticipation of her application to adopt Marisa. Julie dug it out and flipped to the back to look at the instructor biographies. ''Okay, there are three men listed here. Of course, they might be married...''

''Or gay.''

''Right, but here are their names.'' She handed the schedule to Carla, who added the names to the list, then said, ''Oh. I know. The Department of Early Childhood Education at UC. They have to have some single men on faculty. And teachers. We can't list them all, but I'll note it down to be investigated if ol' Frader here doesn't pan out."

Julie frowned and sipped her wine, thoughtful. "I still have to figure out a way to meet them. Frader, I can try to meet after his talk. But the others? I'll have to think of something."

Carla paused, pen in hand. "Maybe you should add experienced daddies to the list." She waggled her eyebrows. "Like that neighbor of yours."

Julie smiled, thinking of Ben. He *was* pretty cute.

Carla said, "Uh-huh. And you've already met that one. And judging by the chemistry I could feel from a mile away, it shouldn't be too hard to move on from here, either." She wrote his name down and underlined it. "I'm betting on him to hold his own." She tore the page out of the notebook. "There you go. The hunt for the world's best dad."

Julie laughed. "I like it."

"I don't know." Carla set the page on a pile of papers on Julie's desk. She picked up her wine as she curled up again on the couch, tucking her feet beneath her. "I still think that whole love thing is going to get in your way."

Chapter Three

Ben helped Joe into his pajamas. "What do you want to read?"

"Edward Overnight."

"*Edward's Overwhelming Overnight?* Oh, that's a good one." Ben set Joe on his feet. "Go get it, and we'll read it."

Joe ran over to the bookshelf and put his hand on the book, first try. He brought the book back and climbed into Ben's lap, and they sat on the bed together, Joe cuddled under Ben's right arm.

"'The telephone rang. It interrupted Edward's story…'" Ben had read the story of Edward, the bear who wasn't ready to spend the night away from home, until he was sick of it. But Joe wanted it every night. Lately he'd taken to sleeping with the book.

This time, after he finished reading, Ben pulled Joe around to look into his face. "Joe, you know you never have to stay overnight anywhere you don't want to, don't you?'' Joe nodded, but he didn't look convinced.

Ben leaned down closer. ''I promise. You will never have to stay anywhere you don't want to stay. Understand?''

Joe nodded again. ''But what about at Grandma's?''

Maggie. He knew it. She was behind this, talking to the poor kid about coming to stay with her. Scaring him out of his wits. Calmly he said, ''Not Grandma's, either.''

''But can I stay there if I want?''

''If you want to?''

''Grandma says if I stay overnight at her house, we can go to Chuck E. Cheese for lunch.''

Ben bit back a smile. Should have known food figured somewhere in all this. ''Is that what you want to do?''

''Can you come, too?''

''Well, probably not. I'd stay here and work.''

Joe thought for a moment. ''Then can *we* go to Chuck E. Cheese?''

Ben laughed. ''Sure, we'll go one of these days.'' He slid Joe under the covers and tucked them snug around his shoulders, then leaned down for a kiss good-night. ''Who's my favorite kid in the whole wide world?''

Joe grinned and wiggled under the covers. ''I am!''

''You're right.''

"An' who's my favorite daddy?" Joe had added this lately, probably with a little help from Maggie. She really did have Joe's best interests at heart. Feeling a little guilty at his earlier anger with her, he grinned at his son. "I am."

"That's *right*." That was Joe's favorite part, and he always added a few decibels for emphasis.

Ben switched on the night-light and turned off the lamp. "Night, Joe. I love you."

In the darkened room, he could see through Joe's bedroom window to Julie's house. Maybe he'd call over there, apologize again for the sandbox incident. Then he saw her friend's car was still parked in the driveway.

Well, no rush. If she'd been dating someone, the guy would have been there today, helping her out. Ben had all the time in the world to get close.

THE FOLLOWING Monday morning, Julie locked the door and led a subdued Marisa across the driveway to Ben's house.

As Julie knocked on the door, she said, "Honey, preschool's going to be okay." Marisa shook her head, and Julie's heart sank. Joe, still in his pajamas, opened the door.

"My dad's upstairs."

"Julie, that you?" Ben came to the top of the stairs, Joe's shoes in his hand. "Joe just needs to get himself dressed." He walked down the steps and handed Joe his shoes. "Now get dressed and get your shoes on, or I'm turning off the TV."

An exasperated sigh from Joe. "Oh, Okay." He grabbed the shoes and trudged into the living room.

Marisa looked up at Julie, anxious, and Julie set a hand on her shoulder. "Go ahead, honey, I'll be right here. I won't leave without you, I promise." She bit her lip as Marisa reluctantly parted from her and slowly followed Joe into the living room. Julie could hear the Rugrats theme playing. Maybe Marisa's favorite show would distract her from her anxiety.

"Cup of coffee? It'll take him a few minutes." Ben shook his head. "I can do it for him, but I've been trying to get him to dress himself in the morning."

"No hurry, we're early. But yeah, I'd love another cup of coffee."

He led her into the kitchen and poured her a cup. "Marisa's first day at preschool. She doesn't seem too excited about it."

That was an understatement. "She's hiding it as best she can, I think, but she's terrified. Thank goodness Joe's school had room for her. It would have been so much worse if she didn't know someone." Julie dropped into a chair beside the table as Ben poured her a cup of coffee and set it in front of her. "I feel terrible. This is really my fault. If I—" She shook her head and took a sip from her mug.

"If you what?"

Julie looked up at him. "If I'd only thought about the ramifications of doing this alone. I had every chance. Everyone and their brother pointed it out to me."

Ben looked mystified.

Julie shook her head in exasperation with herself. "It's a long story, I'm afraid." She gave him a wry smile.

Ben sat down with his cup. "Believe me, it'll take Joe at least ten minutes to get dressed. But don't let me pry."

"Not at all." Julie glanced through the kitchen door into the dining room and living room beyond, where both kids were sitting on the couch absorbed in yet another devious plan by the spoiled-rotten Angelica to ruin the babies' fun. "Marisa and I are just getting to know one another. She still doesn't quite believe that this is for keeps. She was bounced around so much in the past four years."

"So she thinks maybe this whole day-care thing is just another way to get rid of her?"

"I think maybe she does. I've tried to explain that I'd much rather stay with her all the time but that I don't have any choice, I have to work. I don't think she's buying it."

Ben gazed at her, thoughtful, giving her some of his calm. "I'll bet it's pretty important that I pick them up right on time, isn't it?"

Grateful, Julie smiled in relief. "I didn't know

how to bring that up.'' Already he understood a lot about Marisa.

He grinned. He had a dimple immediately to the left of his mouth. Just the one side, giving him a consistently wry smile. ''Afraid it would sound a bit rude to remind me to be punctual? I know how hard you work at being a good mom. If you ever have any other concerns like that, don't worry about being rude, okay?''

''It's just that there were so many obstacles to the adoption, and I never knew, right up until the day the papers were finalized, whether or not it would go through.'' She shook her head in remembered frustration. ''So I didn't know what to tell Marisa.''

''Why was it so difficult? Because you're single?''

''That, and that I work long hours sometimes. And I'm younger than most adoptive parents. When I applied to adopt her, I became an interested party, so I couldn't continue as Marisa's *guardian ad litem.* I'd been representing her needs in court for four years, and now they had to assign someone new, who had to do her own investigation.'' She sighed. ''And Marisa's last foster mother thought the whole idea was nuts.''

''Helpful of her.''

Julie shook her head. ''She did have a point, though. I'd gone over to take Marisa out for the day, and her foster mother told me she and her hus-

band couldn't keep Marisa any longer. She was trying to talk me into fostering Marisa for a few
weeks, so she wouldn't have to go to a temporary
care facility while social services found a new foster home for her.'' Julie swallowed hard as the
memory ate at her. ''I was listing all the reasons it
was a bad idea. And then I heard something out in
the hallway behind us.''

''Marisa?''

Julie nodded. ''I walked into the hall, and she
was sitting there on the steps. She'd overheard the
whole thing. Or, at least, enough to figure out she'd
been rejected again, by both of us.''

The whole horrible scene played out in Julie's
mind as she told Ben the story.

JULIE HAD TAKEN a step toward Marisa and put her
hand up to the little girl's tear-soaked cheek. ''You
heard us talking.''

Marisa had nodded, her dark eyes filling again
with tears.

''What did you hear?''

''I got to go somewhere new.'' She'd sobbed, a
low keening Julie felt in her own chest.

''Oh, sweetie.'' Julie had walked around the railing and up the stairs, climbing to where Marisa sat
midway down the flight. She sat down next to the
little girl and pulled her into her lap, kissing the
part in her shiny dark hair.

''I was good though! I was good! I always picked

up my room at cleanup time, and I tried not to splash too much.''

"Marisa, it's nothing you did.''

"Then why do I got to go somewhere new?''

She hugged Marisa a bit tighter. "Marisa, this could turn out great. Going to a new home means maybe some nice couple might foster you, someone who can adopt you someday.'' It didn't feel right, saying that, but how could she tell the poor kid how unlikely that was?

"When?''

"I'm not sure, exactly.'' Marisa's eyes filled with anxiety again, and Julie kicked herself. For Marisa, uncertainty was the worst of all possible scenarios. "But honey, listen, this next part you're going to like.''

Marisa looked up at her, eyes full of hope, and Julie suddenly realized this next part might not be all Marisa could have hoped for at all.

But she summoned a smile, hoping it would help Marisa see things in a positive light. "Until we find the new foster home, you're going to come stay with me.''

"Oh.'' Marisa looked down again. "For how long?''

"Well, honey, for as long as it takes. Maybe a couple of weeks, maybe a couple of months. I'm going to get you your own bed, and we'll make popcorn every night. And pretty soon, you'll have a great new place to live.'' The words felt so wrong on Julie's lips, she felt queasy speaking them.

Marisa still wouldn't look at her, and as Julie watched, a tear slid down the girl's already wet cheek, and then another. This was more than just anxiety. Julie bent her head down to look into Marisa's face.

Marisa's mouth opened, but before she could speak, she sobbed again. ''How come nobody wants me?''

Julie pulled Marisa close, hugged her tight. Her heart broke again for the little girl. What could she say to her? That someone did want her? That eventually she'd be adopted? She couldn't make promises like that.

Marisa sobbed against her chest, and Julie held her as close as she could.

''I want you, honey. I can't wait for you to come and stay with me.''

If anything, Marisa cried harder. ''Then why don't you want to adopt me?''

Why didn't anyone want Marisa? Suddenly the whole question took on a new significance. It was no longer just rhetorical. It was personal. Why didn't *Julie* want her? And if Julie wanted her, why didn't she want her permanently?

Why didn't Julie adopt Marisa?

There were a million reasons why not. She was too young, she was too busy. She was too broke.

But she was the only person in the world who loved Marisa.

She didn't know anything about child raising.

But she could learn, couldn't she?

She was a single woman, with no immediate prospects. Every child deserved two parents. Every child deserved a mommy *and* a daddy.

But Marisa didn't even have one parent. She didn't even have a permanent foster parent, just a long string of temporary ones. She didn't have anyone. How could one parent be worse than none at all?

Julie couldn't believe she was doing it. She'd never done anything this impulsive in her entire careful life. But she pulled Marisa away so she could look into her face. "I do want to adopt you, Marisa. And I'm going to."

Somehow, she'd fix it.

She could learn to be a good parent. She'd take some parenting classes. Read some books. She'd be the best mom she could learn how to be. And eventually maybe she could fix the daddy situation, too.

Julie looked up in time to see Marisa's foster mother watching them through the banister, her mouth in a shocked O of surprise. She felt a thrill of alarm at the woman's reaction, but she gave Marisa a final squeeze and a kiss. "Go upstairs and wash your face so we can get going."

Julie stood and walked back down the stairs, waiting until she heard the bathroom door close behind Marisa before she turned to Marisa's foster mother. "What?" She heard a half-afraid defiance in her own voice.

"Are you crazy? You?" Julie winced at the scorn in the woman's voice. "Adopt a five-year-old?"

"Why shouldn't I? I love her. Isn't that what matters the most?"

"Have you even given this any thought? You live in a studio apartment, you have no money, you're twenty-five years old, and you've never cared for a child except for trips to the zoo and the aquarium. It's not all fun and field trips, you know. Worst of all, you're single. Do you know how difficult it is to raise a child with *two* parents? And Marisa, with her attachment issues? She needs a full-time mother, not someone who's going to dump her in day care ten hours a day." She'd turned away, disgusted, and Julie had waited alone in the hallway for Marisa to come back downstairs.

JULIE WAS FIGHTING TEARS, just remembering. She looked over at Ben, who had set his coffee cup down while he listened to the story. His eyes held empathy, understanding, and she could have lost herself inside them. "Anyway, she wasn't the only one who brought that up. And they were all right. Marisa needs two parents, so she can have a parent at home with her." She looked up at Ben. "And I'm going to fix that if it's the last thing I ever do as a parent.'' Julie blinked away her tears and gave a self-deprecating laugh. ''I'm sorry, what a story to start off the day, huh? That'll teach you to pry.'' She grinned.

''I'm glad you told me.'' He reached out his hand and set it on top of hers, his palm warm and rough on the back of her hand. She looked up into his face, startled by the small thrill of warmth she felt deep inside, and for a moment they stared into each other's eyes. ''But how are you going to fix—''

From the living room, Joe let out a shriek. ''I can't see! You're in the way!''

Ben's gaze flickered away from her face, toward the noise. ''Hey, what's going on in there?'' He rose, and Julie followed him into the living room, her hand still warm where he'd touched her.

Joe sat on the couch, one sock on, his pajama top off, staring at the screen. Marisa sat beside him, between him and the television, pressed back as far into the cushions as she could.

''Joe, you aren't even dressed yet.'' Ben reached over and snapped the television off.

Joe looked at his father in horror, then threw himself backward on the couch with a shriek. ''No! Daddy, it's not over yet!''

''I know it's not over. I told you as long as you got dressed while you watched, I'd leave it on. You didn't get dressed.''

''I'll get dressed now!''

''Sorry, buddy. That was the deal.'' Ben reached

for a sock, and Joe kicked at his hand, then looked at his father in half-defiant dread at what he'd done.

Marisa gasped and shrank against Julie, and Julie reached a protective, reassuring arm around her daughter.

Chapter Four

Ben straightened and gave Joe a reproachful look. "Joe. That is unacceptable. We do not kick."

Joe slid to the floor, crying. "But I want to watch!"

"Then I'd say you're going about it the wrong way, bub. No TV for you tonight. You can watch it again tomorrow."

Joe shrieked. "You said I could watch tonight."

"And then you tried to kick me."

"No. I want to watch."

"Then you better shape up, and quick, or no television tomorrow, either."

Joe frowned at his father,

Julie quelled her desire to laugh at the child's fierce glower. Marisa still hid her face in Julie's skirt, and Julie felt her tremble, poor kid. She patted her shoulder. "It's okay, honey," she whispered.

Ben continued his reprimand. "Is that what you want? No television tomorrow?"

Joe shook his head.

"Then let's get dressed, and you stop this screaming."

Joe crossed his arms and glared at his father. "Okay, but I won't like it."

Julie could see Ben biting back a grin. She had to bite back one of her own at the expression of exasperated affection on his face.

"That's okay, you don't have to like it. You just have to behave in a civilized manner."

Ben quickly dressed Joe in sweatshirt and sweatpants and worked the boy's shoes on over his socks. "There you go, buddy."

Joe gave a deep sigh. "Okay. I won't do it anymore."

Ben smiled and pulled him into a hug. "Good job. You have fun at preschool, okay? I'll be there to get you and Marisa at five."

Julie felt Marisa make note of that. Bless him.

"At playground time, right, Daddy?"

"Yep."

"Okay. Bye, Daddy. Hug and kiss?"

Joe held up his arms, and when Ben leaned down, he grabbed him around the neck and pulled his cheek near enough to plant a wet kiss on it. "Love you."

Julie smiled. It was so obvious how much they loved each other. She wondered if Marisa could see it, and she peeked at her daughter from the corner of her eye to see her reaction. Marisa was watching wide-eyed.

"I love you, too. See you soon."

"See you soon."

Julie kept her eyes on Marisa during the exchange. Was she getting it? "See?" Julie said. "See how it's okay? Even if Ben gets mad at Joe, he still loves him."

Marisa nodded, but she looked puzzled. At least she didn't seem frightened anymore. Which was a relief. What a roller coaster Marisa was on.

Julie held out a hand each to Joe and Marisa, and the three of them walked across the yard to Julie's car for the trip to Happy Learners.

As soon as they got in the door of the preschool, Joe ran ahead into the classroom. Marisa hung back, clutching at Julie's skirt, peering into the room, taking in the calm colors, the shelves full of toys and books. Julie squeezed her hand and walked with her into the room.

A woman in a smock sat at a low table where two girls Marisa's age were putting together a puzzle. She smiled and waved as she stood, then crossed the room to the door.

"Hi, I'm Barb Daniels. We spoke on the phone last week." She shook Julie's hand, then turned to Marisa and squatted down. "And you must be Marisa. I'm Miss Barb." She held out her hand.

Marisa hid her face in Julie's skirt, and Julie shook her head helplessly. She'd explained on the phone why things might be difficult for Marisa, especially the first day.

Barb pulled her hand back. "Marisa, we're going to have so much fun today. Your friend Joe is here, and lots of other kids."

Marisa pulled her face from Julie's skirt and looked up at her, face pleading. "Mom, but I want to go with you. Please."

Barb tried again. "Marisa, you know what? Your mom told me you like to know exactly what you're going to do during the day, so look over here on the wall." Pointing at a sign on the wall beside the door, she held out her other hand to Marisa. Marisa frowned and stepped back, but she eyed the sign, curious in spite of herself.

Barb casually dropped the offending hand. "See, it says at nine o'clock, we have circle time. That's when we sing and talk about stuff. At ten, we have our snack and then go outside to play. At eleven, we do puzzles and play with blocks and read books. After that, we go to the playroom. Then we have lunch, and then we listen to a story, and then it's quiet time. After that, we draw and work in our journals. Then we either go to the playroom or back outside, and then it's time to go home."

"That's when Ben comes to get you, Marisa," Julie said, rubbing a reassuring hand on Marisa's shoulder.

Marisa bit her lip and looked at Julie. "But what if Ben doesn't come? He might forget."

Julie leaned down. "I promise he won't forget, Marisa."

Marisa looked unconvinced.

Julie wavered, tears burning in her own eyes. Maybe Marisa just wasn't ready yet. Maybe Julie should take her back home, call in to the office and tell them she wasn't going to make it today.

But she remembered what the book said. Julie had read the section three times last night.

> When dropping a child off at school or day care, simply smile cheerfully and tell her to have a good day. Give her a big hug, but don't make a production out of saying goodbye, even if the child does.

Taking a deep breath, Julie pasted on a smile and gave Marisa a hug. "You're going to have so much fun today. And I'll see you back at home."

Tears flowed down Marisa's face. It nearly killed Julie to wave and walk out the door, but she did it.

Then she sat in her car and cried. In the car on the way to work, she called Happy Learners. "How's Marisa?"

"Well, she did cry for a while after you left. Maybe she needs more sleep at night." Julie felt tears in her own eyes. "Try not to worry—this is nothing. Some kids scream and cry and throw themselves on the floor. We'll take very good care of her."

Julie hung up, but she didn't feel much better. Of course, Marisa wasn't showing how upset she really was. Marisa would never act up, never throw a tantrum like Joe had this morning.

Which was beginning to bother Julie.

She was still thinking about it when she walked into the office.

Carla looked up from her keyboard and pulled her Dictaphone headset down. "Hey. Welcome back. How was Marisa's first day at school?"

"Awful. She was weeping from the stress, trembling. I wish I knew what to do." She slid her purse under her desk. "Carla, Marisa never throws temper tantrums."

"So? Lucky you."

"But don't you think she *should* be throwing tantrums, at least occasionally? Have you ever known a kid who didn't?"

"Oh, I see what you mean." Carla stuck her lip out, thinking. "Why do you think she doesn't?"

"Because she doesn't feel comfortable enough with me to lose control? She's worried about what will happen if she does? Worried about what I'll do, that maybe I'll send her away? I don't know. I just don't think it's normal."

"It'll probably just take time." Carla smiled. "And we'll celebrate when she throws her first tantrum, eh?"

"Champagne for everyone."

The phone rang, and Carla picked it up. "Motivation, Inc." She listened for a moment. "May I tell him who is calling?" Another pause, then she hit a button on her phone. "Ed, it's Phillipa Grange." She listened for a moment, then clicked off.

"Great, he'll be on forever. And I'll be hearing it through the Dictaphone. I wish he'd get these phones fixed." Carla pulled the headset back up and listened a moment. "Yep, there's Phillipa. I'll probably be typing out the conversation instead of the dictation."

Julie grinned in sympathy, then turned to her own work.

"Whoa!" Carla had her hand to the headset. "Man, Phillipa's ripping Ed a new one. I told him he needed to call her back last week. He was so freaked out over Cinci Eagle that he was ignoring his messages." She listened a moment more. "Phillipa says it's the last straw. She wants you to be her contact from now on." She paused, listening again. "Ed's trying to soothe her. Oh, bless his heart, he's blaming it on you."

Julie rolled her eyes. No surprise there. Ed was an accomplished scapegoater.

Carla laughed. "Yep, you've apparently lost your mind, some hormonal thing involving the ticking of your biological clock, and decided to join the mommy track. Ed's admitting, shamefacedly, that he's been trying to cut you some slack, and he apologizes for any inconvenience your bout with insanity is causing Phillipa. Oh, wait." She held up a finger, listening, chewing on one side of her lip.

"Phillipa isn't buying, but she's somewhat mollified. Ed should tell you to call her." She laughed. "I can tell he's insulted by being asked to deliver a message, but he's trying to hide it. Oh, they hung up."

Julie laughed, shaking her head. "You are completely shameless."

"But quite handy to have around, don't you think?"

The intercom on Carla's desk buzzed.

"Yes, Ed?"

"Send Julie in, please."

Carla waggled her eyebrows at Julie as she got up. She knocked on Ed's door.

"Come in."

"You wanted to see me, Ed?"

"Yes, Julie. I've just had a troubling conversation with Phillipa Grange."

Julie pasted on a surprised look. "I talked to her before I left for the week and she seemed fine."

He reddened. "Well, now she's not. She's unhappy that there hasn't been any contact during the week you were gone. Call her, and pronto. We can't afford to risk losing that account. Especially not for a simple inattention problem."

Julie gritted her teeth but forced herself to nod in agreement. "Absolutely, Ed. I'll call her right away, make sure she's happy."

"Well, don't make her too happy." He chuckled a little at his own joke. If the client was too happy with what they'd received for their money, you hadn't charged them enough, that was Ed's philosophy. He couldn't stand thinking he might have left something on the table.

He nodded, one short downward motion, satisfied he'd accomplished his goal. "Thank you, Julie. That will be all."

Julie closed the door behind her and leaned over Carla's desk. "Which is another thing! What's with this lord-of-the-manor-dismissing-a-servant stuff he's doing all of a sudden? 'That will be all.' What does he expect me to say to that? 'Very well, milord'?"

"Psht." Carla gave her a look of mock exasperation. "He expects you to walk out backward, bowing slightly. Sheesh, you really don't understand your place, do you?"

Julie laughed and lowered her voice. "No, really, though. I think he's expecting a promotion. He's started dressing better, have you noticed?"

Carla's eyes widened. "And you know what? While you were gone, he had a bunch of long lunches with the brass. Figures, huh? Hey, maybe we'll get promoted, too, this time."

Fat chance of that. "Or we could just end up with a new boss to break in. Again."

"True. But maybe we'd get a really good boss this time."

Julie laughed and picked up her phone. "Okay,

now stop. I have to call Phillipa, and I need to be serious.''

Julie cleared her throat and dialed. ''And no listening in. It makes me stutter when you do that.''

On the other end of the line, the phone rang once.

''Phillipa Grange.''

''Hi, Phillipa. Julie Miles.''

Phillipa gave a nasty laugh. ''Lit a fire under Ed, did I?''

Julie smiled. ''You could put it that way.''

''He tried to blame it on you, you know.''

Julie shot a glance at Carla. ''Well, it probably is my fault. I should have found time to call you from home.''

''Well, water under the bridge. Just don't let it happen again. Here's the problem as I see it...'' She launched into a list of changes she wanted made yesterday. ''When can you get me the revisions?''

Julie looked back over her notes. ''Well, some of it's pretty comprehensive.'' And she couldn't stay late this week, not with Marisa just starting at day care. ''First of next week?''

For a moment, Phillipa didn't answer. ''You know this project is very important to us?''

Julie felt a small thrill of alarm. ''Yes, of course. And it's very important to us, too. Do you need it sooner than Monday?''

Another pause. ''No, Monday's okay. As long as it's perfect by then.''

Julie put the phone down with a sinking feeling in her stomach.

Carla smirked at her. "Well? Everything fixed?"

"I don't know." Julie shook her head. "I'm going to have to work over the weekend as it is. You too, I'm afraid."

"Hey, you can only do the best you can do."

But what if that's not good enough? she thought.

"Que sera, sera."

"Until she fires us." She looked at the clock. "I'm going to check on Marisa again."

Picking up the phone, she punched the number.

"Happy Learners, Miss Barb."

"Hi, Barb, it's Julie Miles again. How is Marisa doing?"

"Well, she's having a rough time, I'm afraid," Miss Barb said. "Really, I wonder if she's vitamin deficient?" Barb sighed and Julie's heart sank. "She has been in tears several times this morning, and she has been asking when she's going to go home."

And it wasn't even lunchtime yet. Poor kid! "Should I come get her?" But if she did that, how in the world was she going to get any work done?

"Well, let's give her a few days. And in the meantime, make sure she's getting enough exercise."

Julie felt torn. Her first instinct was to rush over there, pull Marisa into her arms, reassure her. But maybe Barb was right and she just needed time. Finally she agreed and hung up. She sighed.

"Marisa not doing so great?"

Julie ran her hands through her hair, feeling frazzled. "She's crying on and off. She wants to go home. And she needs more sleep, exercise and vitamins."

Carla laughed. "Oh, an advice giver, huh? Well, I'm sure Marisa will be fine."

Julie wished she was sure.

She managed to keep her mind mostly on her work for the rest of the day, but at five-thirty, she couldn't take any more, even though she knew Ed was expecting her to work late tonight since she'd been off for a week. "Carla, I have some materials to drop off on the other side of town," she said, loudly enough to penetrate Ed's office walls. "I'll just go home from there. See you tomorrow."

"Oh, yes, that stuff for Phillipa," Carla practically bellowed, embellishing the story in a manner guaranteed to keep Ed from asking questions. Julie laughed and waved her thanks on her way out the door.

She hurried home, pulling into the garage behind her house. As she crossed the backyard, she saw a light on inside the open door to Ben's garage. She stopped and poked her head inside. Ben was standing at a workbench against the far wall. "Ben?"

He turned, and his smile at seeing her made her heart sing.

"Where are the kids?"

"They're inside, having a snack. I just stepped out here to check the glue on this chair." He indicated a rocking chair on the bench beside him.

She bit her lip, looking at the windows of the house. "How was she when you picked her up?"

He leaned back against the bench. "She was crying."

Julie felt tears in her own eyes again, and Ben reached out and touched her shoulder, which just made her want to cry more.

"She perked right up, though, soon as she saw me. And now she's happy as a clam, eating her pudding with Joe. I'm sure it'll work out."

Julie nodded and took a deep breath, trying not to think about him touching her, comforting her, because it just made her want to cry more. She blinked, then looked around, noticing the rest of the workshop for the first time. Pieces of furniture—rocking chairs, tables, bookcases—stood in various states of completion on workbenches. Carved mantels, doors and windows, obviously taken from older homes, lined the walls, stacked several deep. The small amount of space left in the center of the room was filled with strange-looking machines on waist-high tables.

She walked over to the rocking chair he'd been working on. It was beautiful—dark wood, with intricate carvings on the legs and chair back. She reached out to touch it. "It feels like butter." She smiled. "You made all these?"

He nodded, running a hand over the wood where her hand had just been, his fingers sliding lovingly along the curve of the wood. "I spend most of the year on construction, but during the winter, I get a chance to work in here a lot."

"You just build these...to build them?"

"Most are contract pieces. People who've seen my work and want me to design and build something for them. And who don't mind waiting until I can get to it."

He was obviously talented. "Why don't you do this all the time?"

He shrugged. "Someday I will. But for now, construction is a reliable paycheck, nine months of the year. With Joe, I don't have the luxury of starving between commissions, and since I only do it three months a year, I can't really build up word of mouth very fast."

She wandered through the room, touching the pieces, marveling at the carving, the bits of whimsy. On a small desk, a shallow space stood open. "What's going here?"

He picked up a piece of wood from the workbench beside the desk. "This'll be a drawer front." He held it loosely, spreading his fingers across the front of it where the grain twisted, his thumb sliding over the spot. "I looked for weeks for just this whorl. It doesn't look like much right now, but when I've got it sanded down and stained, it'll be amazing.''

She pulled her gaze from his hands. ''What an unusual spot for a drawer.''

''It's going to be a secret drawer, hidden in a stretch of trim. That's why I wanted a special graining, to distract the eye.'' He reached to a shelf behind her head and came back with an ornately carved section. He held it up to the space beneath the drawer. ''This is what the skirt will look like.''

Julie had to touch it, as if by touching it she could understand how it had been made. As she did, her hand brushed his, and in that instant she felt his awareness of her. She pulled back, flustered, and turned away.

Across the room were several small carvings on a table. ''Those aren't furniture.''

Ben followed her gaze, then reddened. ''Oh, those are just some stuff I do in off hours.''

She walked over, though he seemed reluctant to have her do so, and picked up one of the pieces. It was a woman's head, beautifully carved, and suddenly she gasped. ''The grain—her face is in the grain!'' She held it up to him. ''How did you do that?''

He took it from her, his hands spreading over it as if he were slightly embarrassed. ''I don't know, actually. I just study the piece of wood, and figure out what's in it, what it needs to get it out. Each piece of wood is alive, unique. There's something of beauty in every piece of wood, something special that makes that piece of wood different from any other. It's the carver's job to discover what that is, to bring it out, to enhance it and encourage it.''

"How did you learn?''

He shrugged. ''I just sort of followed my instincts, I guess. I don't think it's something you can really teach anyone. You have to just work at it, let it develop in you.''

"Just like what's in the pieces of wood, huh? It's in there, waiting to be let out?'' She liked that idea. She liked even more that he thought about such things.

He smiled. ''I guess it is.''

She looked at her watch. ''Which reminds me, I better go check on Marisa.''

Laughing, he followed her to the door. ''That reminded you of Marisa?''

As they stepped outside, she nodded, thinking. ''There's so much inside her, waiting to be let out. All of her childhood trust, I think. I want to help her.'' Tears threatened again, and she laughed. ''You probably think that's pretty silly.''

He stopped, searching her face with his eyes. ''I don't think it's silly at all. I think it's wonderful of you.'' He reached up to her face, stroking away the promise of a tear that had crept onto her cheek, and she realized how close she was standing to him, how aware of him she was. She raised her gaze to his, and for a moment they leaned toward each other.

He was going to kiss her.

And more than that, she *wanted* him to kiss her.

MAGGIE ROBINSON PULLED into her son-in-law's driveway at a little after six-thirty. Perfect timing. She should be able to get an idea of what Ben had served for dinner. Unobtrusively, of course. Though if she found another frozen pizza box in the trash, she was going to say something about it this time. She'd tried giving Ben recipe after recipe, but the indirect approach wasn't working. The man could not take a hint. And it was really too bad, because Joey always ate his good broccoli for her. Why Ben thought he wouldn't eat it, she couldn't figure out. Just lazy, that was the trouble with Ben.

She turned off the engine and retrieved from the passenger seat the newspaper clipping she'd brought with her. Not that Ben would appreciate her trouble in bringing it to his attention. She was just trying to help. And whether he saw it as interference or not, she would never stop trying. Her grandson deserved no less.

She knocked on the front door, and after a too-long moment, Joey opened it. "Grandma!"

"Joey!" She leaned down to pull him into a hug. "How's my best boy?"

"Me and Marisa are having pudding."

"Marisa?" Not another baby-sitter! But, no,

Ben's car had been in the driveway. "Who's Marisa?"

"She's my very, very best friend." He took her hand and tugged her into the kitchen, where a little girl was sitting at the table with a pudding cup in front of her and a good deal of chocolate pudding on her face. "See? That's Marisa. This is my grandma!"

The little girl looked up at her, shy but interested. "You're a grandma?"

Maggie nodded, smiling, charmed by the awe in the child's voice.

Marisa eyed her for a minute, speculative. "Can you be my grandma, too? I don't have one."

Maggie's heart melted. "How about if I'm your pretend grandma? And you can be my pretend granddaughter."

Marisa considered that for a moment. "Can I call you Grandma, though?"

The darling! "Yes, dear, you may call me Grandma." She patted the precious child on the cheek. Then, recalling her mission, she turned to Joey. "Where's your father, dear?"

"He went in the workshop. He said he'd be right back, but he didn't come yet."

"I see." Not that Maggie was surprised that Ben would leave two small children unsupervised in the house. She always hoped he'd do the right thing, and she was always disappointed. "You two come with me. Let's go find Joey's father."

With the children trailing her, she strode through the kitchen—cluttered as usual—to the back door. She opened it, both children behind her.

Ben was standing with some woman on the doorstep of his workshop. Standing too near her, his face too close to her, his gaze locked with hers. Maggie stopped, suddenly cold. Ben looked as if he was about to…to *kiss* her.

Chapter Five

In the back of his mind, his full attention focused on the irresistible nearness of Julie's lips, Ben heard a small sound. Since it didn't seem to be coming from Julie, the part of his brain that was still working in logical fashion decided to ignore it. He leaned closer.

Until Julie pulled away. Dismayed, Ben focused on her eyes again and saw that she was looking at something over his shoulder.

He turned. Maggie stood in the doorway of his house. She had a grip on the door and was trying to pull it shut behind her. Joe cried out from the other side of the door. "Grandma, let us out. I have to go to the sandbox."

Ben reddened under Maggie's accusing glare and turned away from Julie. She stepped back from him just as Joe and Marisa followed Maggie through the door. Joe ran past them as Marisa yelled, "Mom!" and ran to Julie, clinging to her.

Julie hoisted Marisa onto her hip. "Oh, I'm so glad to see you. I missed you."

"I missed you, too." Marisa clung to her neck as if she thought Julie might let go.

Maggie stepped forward, her mouth set as tightly as the bun that perched atop her head. "Hello, Ben."

"Maggie. I wasn't expecting you."

"No, apparently not." She gave him a stiff smile, more a rictus of disapproval, then looked pointedly at Julie, who blushed. He started to extend a reassuring hand to her, then thought better of it and dropped his arm to his side. He cleared his throat. "Maggie Robinson, Julie Miles. Julie's our new neighbor. Julie, Maggie is Joe's grandmother."

Julie, still red, didn't seem to know where to look. She held out her free hand.

After a moment Maggie took it. "Pleased to meet you, I'm sure." Maggie looked anything but pleased.

"Oh. Yes, very pleased to meet you, Mrs. Robinson." Julie looked as if she'd happily jump into any hole that opened up before her.

Maggie's sharp gaze halted its search mission of Julie's face for a moment and focused on a point across the yard. "What's Joey doing?"

Ben turned, for a moment feeling relieved at the distraction. Then he saw Joe, standing next to Julie's sandbox, struggling with his zipper. *Oh, no. Not again.*

Taking a panicked step toward him, Ben called, "Joe. No."

Joe turned his head, then turned back to the sandbox. Ben started after him, covering the twenty yards in a few short seconds. "Joe, I said no."

Joe started to unzip his pants. Maggie gasped. "Oh, dear! Ben, what in the world...?"

Ben grabbed Joe by the arm and turned him around to look into his face. "Joe, what the heck do you think you're doing?"

Joe, his face set in mutinous lines, tried to jerk away. He turned back to the sandbox.

And Ben, past thinking, leaned over, one hand grasping his son's elbow, and gave him a swat on the rear.

Maggie gasped in outrage. He heard a smaller sound of surprise from Julie.

Ben straightened, shocked at himself. Joe turned to look at him, his mouth agape in astonishment. It was hard to tell which of them was more surprised. "Joe, you told me you weren't going to pee in the sandbox again, didn't you?"

The boy nodded and rubbed his behind.

"Then what are we doing out here?" He heard the exasperation in his own voice. Heard the humiliation at having lost control with his son. And in front of Julie.

He heard Maggie say to Julie, "We have to do something. I'm afraid he'll hit him again!"

Joe stuck out his lower lip. "'Cause I'm a cat." His tone of voice added, *As I told you last time.*

You had to give the kid points for a certain consistency in his thinking. Now Ben really did need to laugh. Ben turned his face briefly away from Joe, put a hand to his lips and wiped hard across them, wiping the temptation to smile away. "Joe, time for bed."

Joe's jaw dropped. "Dad! No! It's daytime out!"

"March. Jammies on and in bed. I'll be in to check on you in a minute."

Joe's face got that look that meant a tantrum was coming on.

"Unless you want no more television for another day. Is that what you want?"

Defeated, Joe gave an exaggerated sigh and trudged toward the back door.

"Well!" Maggie was practically twitching in her agitation. "I see I'm just in time with this." She brandished a newspaper clipping in his face. "I was bringing this down for you, but I had no idea you needed it so badly."

He took it. It read Noted Child Psychologist, Author, To Speak On Parenting. He sighed and held the paper up for Julie to see. "Here, it's your guy."

She glanced at the article, then smiled politely at Maggie. "Actually, I was already planning to go hear him speak."

Maggie looked at her more closely this time, a little more warmly. "You're interested in parenting issues?"

Julie nodded. "I'm a new mom." She gave a wry smile. "I figure I need all the help I can get." She smiled into Marisa's face. "Don't I?" Marisa buried her head in Julie's neck.

"Well, at least some parents are still trying." Maggie gave one of her trademark sighs. "These days, you can't count on even that. Maybe you can talk my son-in-law into attending the talk, too. He certainly seems to need it! I'll even baby-sit for both of you, if you'll just make him go."

Julie said, "Oh, that's so kind of you. But Marisa and I couldn't impose."

Maggie shook her head, definite. "No imposition at all. If Ben will go, I'll be happy to do it."

Ben sighed. The woman never gave up. "Maggie, you know it's not my kind of thing."

Maggie sighed again. "Given what you just did, maybe it *should* be your kind of thing. Dr. Frader's most recent book is called *Discipline Without Spanking*."

Figured. He couldn't remember the last time he had spanked Joe—probably since he was a toddler and had run into the street. The woman had some sort of evil genius for showing up when Ben was at his worst as a parent.

And maybe she was right. If Ben couldn't handle his problems with Joe any better than that, maybe

Ben did need to bone up on the whole parenting thing. "Okay, fine, I'll go." He smiled at Julie. "But I won't like it."

She gave him a wry smile, and Maggie's eyes narrowed, watching.

Julie gave Marisa a squeeze. "How was school?"

Marisa shrugged and Julie bit her lip, her gaze shooting to Ben, her eyes now full of worry. His heart went out to her.

"Did you have fun? Miss Barb seems really nice."

Marisa shrugged again, her arms tight around Julie's neck.

Ben searched for something he could say to make Julie feel better. Even Joe sometimes made him feel guilty, and Joe loved going to preschool. "Marisa was out on the playground with the other kids when I got there. She went down the big slide, didn't you, Marisa?"

She pulled her head away from Julie's shoulder and looked into her eyes. "It was scary, but I went down it, and it was fun, too."

The relief in Julie's face from Marisa's small concession wrung at Ben's heart. "I'm so glad you had fun."

"Yeah, but I don't want to go back, okay? It's funner here." She returned her head to Julie's shoulder as if that were the end of the discussion, and Julie's gaze, sparkling with tears, met Ben's again. He could see the helplessness in her eyes, the frustration at not knowing what to do, the need for reassurance.

Maggie cleared her throat, the portent of doom. ''I don't believe children are ready for day care at this age. They need their parents home with them.'' She bent a pointed look on Julie. ''Especially their mothers.''

Julie reddened, obviously dismayed, and Ben willed himself not to shout at Maggie, not to tell her to mind her own damn business. Couldn't she see this was hard enough for Julie as it was? As gently as he could, he said to Julie, ''In a perfect world, we'd all be home with our kids.''

''Well, it seems pretty obvious to me that this world is far from perfect,'' Maggie muttered.

Julie gave Marisa another squeeze. ''You hungry, sweetheart?''

She nodded.

''How about we go home and get some dinner, and you can tell me what you did today?'' She turned to Maggie. ''Again, nice meeting you, and I guess we'll see you soon. See you tomorrow morning, Ben.'' Then she turned and crossed the yard, Marisa tucked securely on her slender hip.

Ben heard her talking to Marisa as she walked away. ''You know what? I was thinking of you all day long.''

WHILE SHE MADE and served dinner, Julie asked Marisa about school. Marisa had put together puzzles, and finger-painted, and written her name on her painting: WARSIA. After admiring how many colors Marisa had used, Julie hung it on the refrigerator. "Now, every day, you can bring me another painting from school, okay?"

Marisa looked down at her plate. Her lower lip poked out and she folded her arms.

"Marisa?" Julie held her breath.

The child's face crumpled, and slowly a silent tear worked its way down her cheek. "Okay, I'll go back. I'll be good." She picked up her fork and slowly started eating again.

Horrified, Julie put down her own fork. "Marisa, it's okay to be upset. It's even okay to be really mad sometimes. It's not being bad to feel mad. I wish I could stay home with you, and it makes me a little mad that I can't, too."

Marisa didn't say anything.

There had to be something else Julie could tell her, something she could do that would reach the little girl.

After Marisa was in bed, Julie walked out onto the patio with a book. The sun set fast, and soon she couldn't see to read. But the balmy night was irresistible, and she was still sitting there when a light appeared in Joe's room next door.

As she watched, Ben followed his son into the room. He held him, close in his arms, and Julie remembered how much she'd wanted those arms around her that day. Before Maggie had interrupted them.

Thank goodness it had been Maggie and not Marisa. Marisa had already grown too attached to Ben. She already saw him as a possible father. What would she have thought if she'd seen Julie in his arms? Or worse, if Julie had been kissing Ben when Marisa came through the door?

Boy, had she wanted to kiss him, though. Her heart picked up a beat as she remembered the feeling. It had almost been irresistible.

But she had to resist. Whatever she did, Julie had to protect Marisa. She might need a father, but she needed stability even more. If Marisa saw a relationship developing between Ben and Julie, and it didn't work out, she'd be devastated. With Ben living right next door, it would be too hard on Marisa. The risks were just too great.

And besides, what about finding a wonderful father, a man who could help Julie avoid making mistakes?

Unwanted, the picture of Ben reaching down to spank Joe filled her mind, accompanied by Maggie's gasp of shock.

Of course, Ben had looked pretty shocked, too.

She looked back at Joe's window. Joe sat in his father's lap, the two of them reading a book together. It was the very picture of a good and loving parent. And she was attracted to him, that was undeniable. She'd have let him kiss her, if they hadn't been interrupted. Her heart raced yet again at the memory of his nearness.

Her body certainly seemed to think he was a reasonable choice.

Well, she didn't have to think about it yet. It wasn't as if she had to make some decision between Ben and all the other men in the world tonight. She just had to make sure Marisa didn't know he was in the running.

And Wednesday, she'd meet Maynard Frader. She'd worry about what came after that when it came.

BEN HELD HIS SON in his arms, enjoying the smell of little boy for a moment or two before he spoiled the moment. It felt so good to just hold the kid. Sometimes it was hard to believe he was real. This little person, this mass of frustrating and intriguing and embarrassing and endearing and amazing personality traits. How could something so small have such a ferocious personality all its own? "Mmm-*mmm!* I like hugs from you."

"Mmm. Mmmm." Joe knew the game. He snuggled deeper into his father's arms and screwed his eyes shut tight. "Mmmmm."

Ben hugged him close a little longer, then pulled the child away slightly and sat him on his knee so they could look each other in the eye. He hated to end a good cuddle—they were becoming more and

more infrequent as Joe grew more independent—
but he couldn't let Joe's behavior go by.

"Joe, I want to discuss the sandbox."

Joe pursed his lips and looked away.

"Look at me."

Joe looked at him.

"The sandbox is off-limits, understand?"

Joe frowned. "But I can dig there. I just can't be
a cat."

"Nope." Ben shook his head. "No digging, either. No sandbox, not until next week."

Joe's lower lip trembled. "But I won't do it anymore." The sandbox was his favorite place to play.

"You said that the first time. No sandbox until
next Monday. When you get home from school
Monday, you can play there. Not until then."

Joe shrieked in protest. He threw himself back
on the bed and howled at the top of his lungs.

Ben gazed at him in resignation. "Joe? If you
throw a tantrum, then I'm not going to be able to
read you a story tonight. Do you want a story?"

Joe quieted immediately and nodded, wiping his
eyes.

"Okay, good. What story?"

"Where The Wild Things Are."

Figured. Ben smiled, wondering again how conscious a four-year-old could possibly be of the messages in books. He read Joe the story of Max, who
was very angry with his mother, then slid him under

the covers, and they performed their good-night ritual before Ben turned off the light.

"Dad?"

"Yes, Joe?"

"I'm not a cat anymore. I think I'm a hyena now."

"A hyena?"

"Yeah. Hyenas don't need to go to the sandbox. They just need to go to the baffroom."

Ben smiled into the darkness. Through Joe's window, he could see his new neighbor still sitting on her patio. The sky was fully dark now, and the soft light from the porch lamp, or maybe from the moon, shone on her hair. As he watched, she reached up to smooth it back from her forehead, her fingers pushing it up off her neck for an instant before letting it drop heavily to her shoulders.

He stole a look at Joe. Already fast asleep. Maybe he'd just go back outside and chat up Julie again, see if they couldn't pick up where they'd left off when Maggie'd interrupted them this evening.

He smiled at the thought and turned back to open the window so he'd be able to hear Joe from outside.

Just in time to watch Julie step inside.

WEDNESDAY EVENING, Julie was dressed and had almost finished feeding Marisa when she heard a knock at the front door. Dropping one last scoop of chocolate ice cream into Marisa's bowl, she glanced at the clock. Just on seven. Ben had said he'd bring Joe and Maggie over around seven-thirty, and then they could leave for the parenting talk.

She pulled open the door and was surprised to see Maggie there alone.

"Hi, Maggie. Come on in."

"I thought I'd come over a few minutes early, let Marisa get comfortable with me." She lowered her voice to a whisper. "Ben talked to me about her. I know she has a difficult time dealing with anything new."

Julie smiled. That was like Ben, to worry about Marisa. "That's so considerate of you, Maggie."

"And I wondered if perhaps she might be more comfortable if we stayed over here? Joey doesn't care one way or the other."

Julie nodded. "That might make a real difference to her, actually. Good idea."

Maggie followed Julie into the kitchen. "Marisa, you remember Mrs. Robinson, don't you?"

Marisa looked up from her ice cream. She nodded. "You're my pretend grandma."

Julie reddened. "Honey, a grandma is the mother of a mommy or daddy. My mother died, so that's why you don't have a grandma."

Marisa nodded, solemn. "Some kids even have two grandmas."

"To have two grandmas, you need to have two parents." The minute it was out of her mouth, Julie regretted it.

Marisa nodded, definite, as if she'd already given this some thought. "That's why I need a daddy." She looked at Maggie. "If Mommy married Ben, then would you be my real grandma?"

Maggie's lips tightened, and bright spots of color appeared on each cheek, but she answered Marisa gently. "I think a pretend grandma is just as good as any other kind."

Julie reddened. Things had at least been marginally less embarrassing when Marisa had spent her days with her face hidden in Julie's skirt. Hurriedly she said, "Marisa, if you're done with your ice cream, why don't you run up and brush your teeth, honey? And bring down your pajamas so you can get ready for bed when Mrs. Robinson says."

Marisa dropped her bowl into the sink with a clatter and they heard her run up the stairs.

Julie turned to Maggie. "Thanks, Maggie. That was very kind of you. I'm afraid she's going to hold you to it, though, this pretend grandma thing. I hope you don't end up regretting it."

Maggie shook her head, definite. "I hope she does hold me to it. What I said was the truth. I wish I had a dozen grandchildren." She smiled, a bit sadly. "But that's neither here nor there. Now, tell me everything I need to know about Marisa."

"Well, she usually goes to bed around nine-thirty."

"Goodness, even on school nights? I'll see if I can't get her down by nine, at least. My grandchildren need their rest.'' She crinkled her eyes, smiling.

"And if she gets hungry again, I usually give her a bowl of Cheerios before bed…''

"Oh, I don't mind fixing something hot. So much nicer to go to bed on a warm tummy.''

Julie thought for a moment. ''Well, I think there's some soup in the cupboard.…''

"Don't worry about a thing. I'll poke around a bit, come up with something healthy for the kids. Now, where's your list of emergency numbers?''

By the time Julie had scrounged up a piece of paper and found the pediatrician's phone number, the number for the emergency room at Children's, and the number of the dental clinic, there was another knock on the door.

Julie handed the finished list to Maggie on her way to answer it. ''I can't thank you enough for driving all this way to take the kids.''

"Oh, it's my pleasure. I love taking care of children. And I'm very good at it. So you just go and learn as much as you can, and don't worry about a thing. I'll have everything shipshape by the time you get back.''

BEN KNOCKED AT THE DOOR, then pushed it open for Joe just as Julie came through the kitchen door. She was outlined by the kitchen light behind her, and Ben took the opportunity to admire her without being obvious. She was wearing a long-sleeved

T-shirt made of some white silky material and a long, wrinkly looking skirt that moved when she did. Her calves flashed at him as she turned to speak to Maggie, her feet in strappy sandals that seemed way too bare for propriety. Since when had almost-naked *feet* become so ridiculously sexy?

As she crossed to him, he glanced behind her to where Maggie was standing, peering through her reading glasses at a piece of paper. He leaned over and lowered his voice. "Been Maggie-d, I see? Would that be your list of emergency numbers she's memorizing?"

Julie bit her lip on a shamefaced smile, and he watched, fascinated, as her teeth sank into the flesh of her lip. "But, Ben, she's right. I should have had a list already, for any baby-sitter."

"Just don't let her make you feel like the world's worst excuse for a mother. She's good at that."

From her blush, rosy across her cheeks and touching the lobes of her ears, he could tell that's exactly how Julie had been feeling, but she defended Maggie. "I'm sure she means well."

"Oh, I know she means well. She's a very loving and generous person. The perfect grandmother. Seriously, I don't know what I'd do without her." He gave a wry smile. "With Maggie, you can be absolutely confident the kids will be safe and well protected from all harm."

"What do you mean by that?"

He lowered his voice even more so that she was

forced to lean near him, so he could whisper in her ear, although Maggie had walked back into the kitchen with both kids. He smelled the nearness of her in the light scent of her hair. "My wife, Rose? Never climbed a tree—she might fall out. Never carved a jack-o'-lantern—she might cut herself. Had training wheels on her bike until she was almost ten. And when she was invited to sleep over at a friend's house? First she was too young. Then, suddenly, she was too old for such nonsense."

Julie frowned, uneasiness in her eyes. "Do you think she'll encourage Marisa's fearfulness?"

He shook his head, definite. "I don't think she'll be encouraging her to climb any trees, but she isn't going to be telling Marisa that mommies don't come back to pick up their kids from day care. And that's the kind of thing Marisa is afraid of."

Slowly Julie nodded, and she cut her gaze to him, her blue eyes sharp on his as she smiled. "You're right," she said.

"Don't sound so surprised," he teased her gently. "And even if I were wrong—which of course is impossible—she's only going to be here a couple of hours. What disaster could even Maggie wreak in that much time?"

MAGGIE WATCHED JULIE AND BEN walk across the yard toward Ben's truck. Her eyes narrowed as Ben opened the door for Julie and placed a casual hand on her elbow as she climbed up into the cab.

Ben was interested in her, that much was certain. That was no good.

She turned to the children. "What shall we do?"

Joe said, "Legos!"

Marisa said, "Barbies!"

Maggie smiled. She didn't care what anyone said, little boys and little girls were just *different*. She said, "Okay, first we'll play Legos, then we'll play Barbies."

Joe widened his eyes at her, horrified. "I'm not playing Barbies!"

Marisa bristled. "Then I'm not playing Legos!"

Maggie held up her hands. "Then we'll play both at once." Her knees creaking, she settled on the floor. "Joe, you and I can build a house. Marisa, the Barbies can live in the house. What should they wear?"

Marisa and Maggie put one outfit after another on the two Barbie dolls Marisa owned. Both dolls and all the clothing was obviously brand-new. "Marisa, did your mommy give you these?"

The child nodded. "I didn't have one before."

Maggie nodded in approval. "Mommies are good that way, aren't they?"

"Yes. But we need a daddy, too."

Maggie watched her, trying for a casual tone. "Well, yes, it's better to have a daddy, too."

"I want Ben for my daddy."

Joe frowned. "He's my daddy."

"He could be my daddy, too."

Maggie shook her head. "I think he has his hands full just being Joe's daddy," she said as gently as she could.

She wasn't surprised the child was getting such ideas, given what she'd witnessed the other day.

Later that night, after Marisa was tucked into bed and Joe was asleep in the master bedroom, Maggie picked up the sheet with the emergency numbers Julie had written down for her. She thought maybe she'd post it on the refrigerator for her—it wouldn't do to lose it; the next baby-sitter might not think to ask for it, and then what if there were an emergency?

There wasn't a free magnet on the refrigerator, so Maggie decided to leave the list on the desk. Reminding herself to make sure before she left to tell Julie where it was, she carried it over to the desk.

She started to set it on a pile of papers there when something caught her eye. Holding her glasses in place, she bent closer.

"The World's Best Dad Candidates." She picked up the piece of paper and read over it.

Ben's name was on the list.

Maggie straightened. Well, why shouldn't Julie be interested in Ben—he was certainly interested in her. And, Maggie understood men had needs. It had been two years since Rose's death, and Ben hadn't dated anyone as far as Maggie knew.

But the real question was: how would this affect Joe?

Maggie had a certain idea in mind of what kind of mother would be good for Joey. Joey was a handful. He needed someone mature, someone careful, someone who could devote her full attention to him. Julie was a nice girl, but she was much too young, maybe even flighty. Making a list of candidates for fathers for her daughter, for heaven's sake. And she had a daughter almost the same age as Joey, a daughter who had deep emotional needs.

How much time and energy could a woman with a daughter like Marisa possibly have left for Joey?

And, interestingly, Julie seemed to recognize that herself. All the other names on the list were men who could be considered parenting experts. Men who could help her with Marisa.

Obviously Julie was looking for something in particular. And good for her. That was as it should be.

But why in the world was Ben on the list? He couldn't be considered a parenting expert by any stretch of the imagination. Just the opposite, in fact.

Julie was thinking with something other than her head. Not that any woman could blame her for that. Maggie knew what was what, and even a mother-in-law could tell Ben was attractive.

Perhaps all Maggie had to do was make sure Julie saw Ben for what he really was—well-intentioned, certainly, but no Dr. Spock.

Maggie sat back and began to plan.

JULIE FOLLOWED BEN into the auditorium, hurrying to find seats just as the room was darkening.

A white-haired woman stood at the podium, bragging about the speaker, finally saying, "Maynard Frader has been writing parenting columns for the *Cincinnati Enquirer* for ten years. He has a doctorate in Child Development. Please welcome Dr. Frader."

Dr. Frader, in a tweed jacket with patches on the elbows, rose from his chair to welcoming applause. Julie recognized him from his picture, which had actually been a pretty flattering one, now that she saw him. In person, his eyes seemed closer together, his mouth pinched. He held himself very, very erect, and as he crossed the stage, his steps were small and precise. At the podium, he stood stiffly waiting for the room to quiet. She supposed it was the way he moved that made him seem so fastidious.

No matter, it was his ideas that were important, not the way he looked. She glanced at Ben, who leaned over to whisper, "Yeah, he looks like he gets down on the floor to play with toddlers all the time."

Dr. Frader cleared his throat. "Thank you for having me." He glanced at his notes. "Possibly the greatest challenge for the American parent is that of discipline. When to discipline, how to discipline.

How to insure consistency in discipline. More important still, how to help the child learn to discipline himself.''

As Frader talked, Julie had a hard time listening to him, because every time he said anything, Ben would lean over next to her and tell her something Joe had done that didn't seem to fit. Every time Ben whispered in her ear in the darkened auditorium, she had the strangest desire to turn her face to his.

Which would have put her lips practically against his.

Which she couldn't stop thinking about.

But she really needed to, because obviously Ben wasn't getting the whole point of the speech. With an effort, she concentrated on what the doctor was saying. That children were to be guided along the adventure of developing self-discipline. That the best way for children to learn to discipline themselves was not through overt adult intervention but through learning the consequences of their own actions. An organic approach.

''I wonder how he'd feel about Joe learning the consequences of, say, drawing with crayon on the notes for his speech five minutes before he had to go onstage?'' Ben whispered in her ear. ''Did I ever tell you about the blueprints Joe drew on? Luckily the home owners had six.''

For a moment she thought he'd said ''had sex.'' Then she realized that couldn't be right. ''Six blueprints?'' Still feeling confused, probably because she was having a difficult time thinking, she turned slightly to look at him. He was staring into her eyes, and she quickly looked away, back toward the front of the room.

She felt him shake his head, felt him laugh softly into her ear. ''Six kids of their own. They were very understanding.'' His breath was warm on her neck, and she held her head very still, because if she moved again, even a tiny bit, she knew her hair would brush his lips. The thought made the hairs on her neck rise, and she had an insane desire to do it, right here in public, to drop her head just that fraction of an inch toward his face so that her hair, maybe her ear, would brush lightly against him. So she held herself very rigid to keep from giving in.

Thankfully the talk wasn't a long one. Julie was afraid she wouldn't remember a thing the man had said.

Well, she'd just have to fake it. Because it was time to start putting her plan into action.

She turned to Ben. ''I want to talk to him for a few minutes. Do you mind?''

His eyebrows shot up, but he shook his head. ''Not at all.''

She grinned. ''Thanks.''

And then she took a deep breath and stood up.

BEN HAD NO IDEA what had just happened. One minute, he was practically nibbling on Julie's ear and enjoying himself immensely, the next minute she was walking over to talk to the overstuffed idiot at the podium.

He watched in stony silence as Julie smiled at that pompous windbag Frader, held out her hand in introduction, leaned toward him, laughed at something he said and flipped back her hair.

Flipped back her hair?

Ben frowned and rose to his feet.

Chapter Six

Things were swimming right along, Julie thought. Maynard was charming. Well, in his own way. And he was a perfect gentleman. And he seemed to be picking right up on all the signals she was throwing out. She hadn't flirted this obviously since she was in high school. She must have gotten better at it since then, because Maynard was definitely understanding her better than any football player ever had.

She smiled at Maynard again. "I'd love to talk to you about this some more." While she was flipping back her hair for about the third time, Maynard's eyes fastened on something over her left shoulder. She suddenly felt a little awkward, and she turned to see Ben standing there.

"Oh, hi!" Why did she feel as if she'd just been caught doing something she shouldn't?

He smiled, his mouth tight, his eyes on Maynard. "Just thought I'd wander over to see what you two were talking about so intently."

Maynard turned to Julie, one eyebrow raised in question. "And this would be your…"

She felt herself blush. "Oh! My neighbor, I'm sorry. Maynard, Ben Harbison."

Maynard smiled and placed a hand on her shoulder for a moment, rubbing a little in a tiny circle as if to reassure her. "Not at all." He held out his other hand to Ben, and the two shook. Then Ben reached toward her. She thought he was going to place his hand on her back, but he stopped a few inches from touching her. The skin at her backbone just below her waist tingled as if he had touched her, and she blushed again. Why was she doing all this blushing? All she was doing was talking to the man.

Well, no, actually, she'd been trying to pick the man up. But that should be okay, she thought, detecting a whiff of defiance in her thoughts. This wasn't a date she was on with Ben.

Was it? She looked up at him. He was eyeing Maynard with ill-concealed dislike. Maybe Ben thought it was a date. She thought about the way he'd been whispering to her, the way she'd felt with his breath teasing her ear.

Maybe it hadn't been such a good idea to bring Ben along. Maynard rubbed her shoulder again. Ben shifted his body toward her.

Oh, boy. Better get out of here. She turned to Ben. "You're right, though, we'd better get back before your mother-in-law thinks we've run off together." She felt a blush start again at her choice of phrasing, and quickly turned back to Maynard to hide it.

She smiled, held out her hand to him, and he took it, giving her a smile that excluded Ben from their little group of two. It wasn't a very pleasant smile, but she pushed the thought aside. She was sure the expression on Ben's face wasn't all that pleasant, either.

Maynard handed her a card. "Why don't we further discuss this privately? Over coffee, perhaps?" Another rub on the shoulder. "Happy to help, of course."

She nodded, feeling unaccountably uncomfortable, and he gave her shoulder one last pat, then greeted the next person in line.

She turned away without looking up at Ben again. "Okay, I'm ready." She held her head up as they walked out of the room together.

As he opened the door of the truck for her, Ben said, "So what was all that about?"

She looked at him, all innocence. "What was all what about?"

"Your little talk with Frader. The way he was pawing you."

"He wasn't pawing me!" He probably *had* touched her shoulder a little too often, though, if she was honest with herself. Probably he was just nervous, with Ben hovering.

"Your date tomorrow?"

"I'm not sure I'd call a cup of coffee and a discussion of parenting issues a date."

She tried to come up with something to talk about on the way home, but Ben only answered in distracted monosyllables. Finally, in exasperation, she flipped on the radio and listened as the Reds beat the tar out of the Dodgers in a spring training game.

BEN WAS RELIEVED when Julie turned on the Reds game. That, he could listen to with ten percent of his brain and still leave the rest free to figure out what was going on. For some reason he couldn't do that when Julie spoke to him. She seemed to put out some special sonar only he could hear. He'd just get thinking, and she'd say something, and as soon as he heard her voice, most of his mind was focused on her. It was ridiculous.

And he had some serious thinking to do. Strategizing, really.

It was obvious to him that Julie had been flirting with that Frader idiot.

Julie denied it, but she'd accepted a date with the guy. She might deny it was a date, but Ben knew what Frader was doing, all that touching her to mark his territory. Frader hadn't yet mastered the technique, apparently. He was still doing that shoulder-rubbing crap. Even back in high school Ben could have told him women found that annoying.

Okay, so something was going on, and Julie was saying it wasn't.

Ben could push it, but what would that get him?

So he'd go along with it. If she wanted to ignore it, so could he. He'd just ignore the two of them right back in the direction they'd been heading on Monday before Maggie interrupted them.

For a minute, the thought of that moment distracted him from any more strategizing, the baseball game and driving. He almost ran a stop sign. Luckily Julie made a noise and snapped him out of his thoughts.

When they walked into Julie's house, Maggie was in the living room reading.

Slipping a bookmark carefully between the pages, Maggie slid the book into her bag. "Marisa's in her bed. She said she wanted to sleep on the couch with Joey, like Ben let her," she said, with a stern glance at Ben, "but I told her we sleep in beds, not on couches. And certainly not together! They're much too old for that. I put Joey down on your bed, I hope that's okay. Oh, and I washed her pj's for you before I put them on her. I thought it was best."

As Julie reddened in embarrassment, Ben bristled. Maggie could turn a helpful gesture into an implied criticism like no one he'd ever met. "I'm sure they were just fine."

Maggie gave him an amused glance. "Coming from a man who thinks dirt doesn't exist until it's visible, that shouldn't surprise me.'' She leaned closer to Julie and said in a conspiratorial whisper, ''You and I know good parents care about these things, don't we?'' She nodded her head in agreement with herself.

Julie looked a little stricken, but she said, ''That was so considerate of you. Thank you, and thanks again for taking both kids.''

''My pleasure. Now I'm going to run. Don't want to get home too late, when I've got bridge tomorrow.'' She picked up her purse and her bag, put on her coat and left.

Finally. Ben turned to Julie. ''There's something to be said about coming back home after the kids are already asleep. Mind if I have a beer before I retrieve Joe?''

She smiled. ''My thoughts exactly. Let me just go check on the kids real quick.''

''Beer for you, too?''

''Thanks.'' She trotted up the stairs, and as soon as she was out of sight he sprang into action. He grabbed them each a beer and a glass, then turned off the kitchen light as he left the room so that the living room was lit only by the floor lamps Maggie had turned on. Then he draped his jacket over the seat of the chair, set the glasses on the coffee table, and was sitting smack in the middle of the couch when she came back down the stairs.

He hadn't lost his touch. She didn't even hesitate

at the chair, just picked up her beer and sat down beside him.

Taking a sip, he leaned back on the sofa, his shoulder very near her own. "Oh, that's good. Sometimes I honest-to-God yearn for the end of the day and a cold one."

She smiled and turned to face him. "I know what you mean. Sometimes I'm so tired, I wish Marisa would take a nap just so I could."

"I always tell myself to go to bed after Joe gets to sleep. But I enjoy the time alone so much, I find myself sitting through Letterman just because it feels good not to have anyone asking questions ninety miles a minute."

Julie laughed. "That's Joe, all right. Did I tell you what he asked me the other day?"

He shook his head, turning his face to hers so that they almost could whisper to each other.

"He asked me how come cats don't use the toilet."

Ben laughed. "This must have been before he decided he was a hyena, instead. What did you tell him?"

"I told him some cats did. Only really smart ones, though."

"What did he say?"

She smiled. "I don't think he believed me at first, but I did once train a cat to use the toilet. Mrs. Malloy absolutely refuses, but I had a Siamese that picked it up just like that. So then I asked him if he was still a cat.''

''And?'' She turned her face away for a moment to take a sip of her drink, and he watched her tip her head slightly back, her throat moving smoothly as she sipped and swallowed, a lock of hair falling away from her cheek to expose her ear.

She turned back to him, her face close to his. ''He told me he was a cat, but not a very smart one.'' She smiled. ''What a kid!''

He stared into her eyes, holding her gaze with his own for the briefest moment, then leaned closer. And then he kissed her.

For a moment she didn't move. Then her free hand strayed up to his face. As she touched him, the awareness of her fingers on his skin pulled him closer to her. He pressed into the kiss. And for a moment, he thought of nothing but the feel of her lips, her shoulder, her fingers against him. He could feel her as if she were a part of him.

They pulled apart for a moment to meet each other's eyes, and he knew the shocked look on her face mirrored his own. ''Julie,'' he whispered, and leaned in to meet her lips again, to renew that intensity, and she turned her mouth up to him.

''Daddy?'' From the top of the stairs behind them came a muffled sound. Then, ''Daddy? It's dark!''

Joe.

Julie pulled away from him, her eyes searching

his once again. The small pulse at the base of her jaw fluttered beneath his thumb as he cupped her head, her hair falling over his hand.

Not taking his eyes from hers, he called softly. "Down here, Joe. Everything's okay."

She sat back, away from him, and he felt the loss of the warmth of her nearness. She gave him a small smile, wry, regretful. "He'll be down here in a minute."

He nodded, reluctant, but she was right. "I guess I'd better get him home." He stood and climbed the stairs to where Joe was standing in the hall, blinking sleepily, still clutching a pillow from Julie's bed. He set Joe onto his shoulder, and when he got back downstairs, Julie had taken the empty glasses into the kitchen, the bright light from the kitchen's overhead lamp flooding into the living room.

She walked back out into the living room, the light behind her framing her for a moment. "Good night, Joe. See you in the morning."

Joe murmured sleepily against Ben's shoulder as Ben retrieved his jacket from the chair and wrapped it around his dozing son.

He met her eyes again. "Good night."

She smiled. "Night."

The door closed behind him, and he felt shut away from her, wished he could have stayed inside in the warmth with her.

But it hadn't been a total waste. That was some kiss, what there was of it.

Top that, Frader, he thought as he stepped off the porch. And in the cool darkness of the short walk home, he smiled to himself.

THE NEXT MORNING AT PRESCHOOL, Marisa clung and wept. Barb suggested less sugar in her diet.

When Julie walked through the door at work, Carla handed her a pink message slip before she even got to her desk. She struggled to speak through a bite of bagel. "Phillipa's on the warpath. Now she says she needs that proposal this morning instead of Monday."

Julie groaned. "There's no way on earth. The printers have it."

"Oh, you'll calm her down. She just gets in these panics." Carla took another bite of her bagel and set it on a napkin on her desk.

"She reminds me a lot of Ed that way."

"I know. I think they're twins, separated at birth. Only wait, that can't be, because where's the good twin?"

Julie laughed in spite of herself as she picked up the phone.

"Phillipa Grange, and this better be Julie Miles."

Julie fought the urge to sigh. "Hi, Phillipa," she said, trying for cheery. "I got your message. What can I do for you?"

"You can get me that proposal, ASAP. Sorry for the rush." She didn't sound very sorry.

Julie took a deep breath. "Phillipa, I hate to let you down, but the final version is still at the printer's. I'll get you everything I have, but I'm afraid it's still in draft form."

Phillipa was silent for a long moment. "Well, if that's the best you can do, I guess it'll have to do. Honestly, though, I'm surprised you can't get this done any faster. You used to be able to turn stuff around for me in two or three days."

Two or three days of twenty-hour shifts would have done it this time, too, but Julie couldn't work those kind of hours and be any kind of mom to Marisa. "Phillipa, I'm really sorry. When the proposal comes back from the printer's late today, I'll courier it over to you."

"Won't do me any good. I'm leaving town at noon for Vermont. Getting in the last of the skiing."

Aha. Julie glanced over at Carla, who had her headset on. Carla rolled her eyes, and Julie had to cough to cover a nervous laugh. "Well, how about if I overnight a copy of the final proposal to you there?"

Phillipa sighed. "So I get to work this weekend, because you didn't put in the hours this week? Fine, let's do it that way. I don't appreciate it, though."

Julie got the address and hung up. "She isn't happy."

"Yeah, I heard." Carla made a wry face. "Hey, you can only do the best you can do."

Julie nodded and picked up the phone again. "I'm going to check on Marisa." She got Barb on the phone. "How are things going?"

Barb sounded stressed. "Marisa's finally stopped crying, but she got Jennie and Megan so upset that now they're crying."

In the background, Julie could hear them. Dismayed, she asked, "What do you think we should do?"

"Well, some kids just take a little more time than others. But if she hasn't gotten used to the situation in the next couple weeks, we may have to think about other options."

"Other options?" It didn't sound good. Julie didn't have many other options. "Like what?"

"Maybe bringing her in for half days for a while."

Julie's heart sank. "But I have to work full-time."

"Well, let's not borrow trouble. Maybe it'll work itself out."

As Julie hung up, Carla said, "Problems with Marisa?"

"She's got all the other kids crying now."

"Yeah, crying is contagious. Hey!" Carla waggled her eyebrows at Julie. "I have a great idea! This is the perfect time for you to call that expert, what's-his-face, Fader or whatever. Ask him for advice."

Julie made a face. "Don't you think that's a little, um, obvious?"

"Obvious schmobvious. What do you care? You give him the opportunity to ask you for a date. If he doesn't do it, you'll know he's not interested, and you can move on to the next candidate. Right?"

Julie chewed her lip and stared at her friend. "I kissed Ben last night."

Carla pulled off her headphones. "You did *what?* And you didn't say anything? You wench! Tell."

Julie thought about the kiss. It was the briefest of moments, and yet it was such a perfect moment. "No, it's too corny.

"Corny! Corny how?"

"You'll laugh."

"Of course I'll laugh. Tell me anyway."

Julie laughed herself, then thought for a moment, her eyes losing focus as she put herself back in the moment. "For a moment, while I was kissing him, I thought the rest of the world had dropped away. It wasn't just that I didn't notice anything else. There *wasn't* anything else. It was just…gone."

"Wow." Carla's eyes sparkled. "Love." She grinned. "Does this mean you've given up the marrying-Dr.-Spock idea?"

That brought Julie back to the here and now.

"Not with Marisa crying all day at preschool. Give me that phone." She pulled Maynard's card out of her purse. "Okay, here goes nothing." She dialed the number, and in a few minutes, his assistant clicked her through.

"Certainly I remember you," Maynard replied. "Delightful, of course. I'd be more than happy to talk to you, but why don't we do it over dinner. Let me see, I'm free tonight, then not again for another two weeks. Busy speaking schedule. The book, of course."

Julie covered the mouthpiece. "Baby-sit for me tonight?"

Carla shrugged. "Sure, why not?"

Turning back to the phone, Julie said, "Okay, tonight it is. Eight o'clock?"

He hemmed for a moment. "Let's make it seven. I prefer to eat early. Digestion, of course."

Julie gave him her address and they hung up. "Well, that was easier than I thought."

"See? He was probably wishing he could figure out how to get ahold of you. Why do you ever doubt me?"

When Julie got home that evening, she hurried over to Ben's to pick up Marisa.

"You look exhausted." Ben said when he opened the door.

"Bad week." She looked past him into the living room. "Kids outside?" At his nod, she asked, "What did Barb say when you picked them up? I tried to call late this afternoon, but she was tied up.''

''She said Marisa went up and down. She'd seem to get involved in something, seem to be having fun with the other kids, and then something would remind her and she'd get upset again.''

Julie thought for a moment. ''So she *did* have fun, at least part of the time.''

''That's what it sounded like to me. Julie, I think this is really just something you're going to have to let her go through.'' He looked at her, face intent, gray eyes full of sympathy. ''I know how much you want to, but I don't think you can solve this problem for her.''

Which was probably the heart of the matter. ''You're right. It kills me. I feel so helpless. If I could find a way to make it just a little bit easier, I'd feel I was doing my job.'' The thoughts of how impossible the job of parenting sometimes seemed, of how imperfectly equipped Julie considered herself to be sat like a ball of lead in her stomach. A familiar ball of lead.

''You did make it easier. You put her into preschool with Joe so she would know someone. You carpool with me, so she knows the person picking her up.''

''But she's still upset. I should be doing something about it.'' Julie paced across the living room, agitated. ''Barb thinks I should consider cutting her hours at day care. You and Carla think I should give her a chance to get used to it. Maggie thinks it's awful I leave her all day. Can't you people make up your minds?'' She gave a short laugh. ''I just want to fix it, that's all.''

''Of course you do. You're a parent. That's how parents feel.'' He watched her for a moment. ''I wish I could fix it for Joe so he had his mother back. I can't fix it.''

She stopped pacing and turned toward him. ''Does he miss her?''

Considering, he shook his head slowly. ''Not *her,* exactly. He doesn't remember her. He was barely two when she died. But he misses the idea of having a mother. The other kids all have one, and he wants one, too.''

Julie thought of Marisa and nodded. ''Marisa wants a father desperately, and she never even knew her own....'' She swallowed to clear her throat. ''How much harder that must have been on Joe. On both of you.''

His laugh sounded of remembrance. ''It wasn't easy. It was amazing how difficult even the most everyday things became as soon as there was only one person doing them. Just trying to fold laundry with a two-year-old nearby who needed supervision was a major production. Do you have any idea how long it takes to sort socks when you have to get up every five minutes to follow a toddler out of the room? I finally gave all his socks to Goodwill and bought all plain white ones.'' She laughed, and he smiled. "The only thing I can tell you is that, yes, you and Marisa will get through this."

Joe ran in, covered in mud and trailed by Marisa, who was only slightly cleaner. "Look, Dad! We found a puddle! It was right behind the garage!"

His father gave an exaggerated groan. "Bath time, bub."

Julie hugged Marisa, trying to avoid the muddy parts. "You too, mud girl. After dinner, Carla's coming over to stay with you for a little while, won't that be fun?"

Marisa stiffened. "Where are you going?"

"I'm going out for a bit."

"Why?"

"Well…" Julie blushed a little. "I'm just meeting someone, that's all."

From the corner of her eye, she saw Ben shoot her a glance. "Dr. Frader, I presume?"

She nodded, still looking at Marisa.

"Coffee?"

"Dinner, actually." She looked up at him, unable to resist the urge.

He studied her for a moment. "I'll be happy to take Marisa, if it would help."

"Oh, Carla doesn't mind—"

He shook his head. "It's got to be a lot more inconvenient for her than it is for me."

She didn't like the idea. Marisa was so attached to him already. And Julie was starting to get attached, too. In more ways than one, she thought, thinking again about that kiss.

She looked at him from under her lashes. He was watching her, and she felt a prickle of excitement, her heart picking up a beat as she felt the heat in his eyes. She knew he was thinking about that kiss, too.

Oh, this situation was uncomfortable in the extreme.

But Carla did live almost half an hour away.

''Please, Mom!'' Marisa clutched at her waist, her gaze fixed on Julie's face.

''Okay,'' she said slowly. ''Thanks, Ben, I really appreciate it.''

He shrugged, overcasual. ''That's what neighbors are for. I'll come get her. What time?''

''Seven.'' She herded Marisa home for a quick bath and dinner.

Julie was putting the finishing touches on her makeup when the doorbell rang. That would be Ben, coming to get Marisa for the evening. Thinking about seeing him, she stepped back from her mirror and eyed herself critically.

Then she caught herself.

She wasn't dressing for Ben. She was supposed to be dressing for Maynard, if anyone.

The idea didn't have nearly as much appeal, though. She really couldn't work up any enthusiasm for watching Maynard for his reaction.

Bad sign.

Well, maybe Maynard was the type who grew on you. She gave her dress one last twitch and headed for the stairs.

BEN AND JOE WAITED under the porch roof out of the soft rain for a moment before Marisa tugged open the door, backing away from it step by step to pull it open for them, peeking around it. He smiled at her. "Your mom ready?"

She turned to look at the stairs. "She's upstairs. She's wearing a dress. A beautiful, beautiful dress."

A dress, huh?

And then he wasn't thinking anymore because Julie was walking down the stairs toward him, wearing the dress in question, and his throat tightened up.

It was a very interesting dress.

Not that there was anything so unusual about it. Other than the color, a blue that somehow did something to her eyes. And the hem, cut just to where her thighs promised to swell. And the material, something soft that clung to curves and floated on smooth skin, mesmerizing, the movement of it promising a glimpse of something not quite forbidden if he allowed himself to watch patiently.

He tore his gaze from her hemline, glancing at her face to see if she'd noticed him staring. She smiled serenely, and he suspected she'd noticed very well, thank you.

He opened his mouth to tell her how beautiful she was, but before he could make a total fool of himself, the doorbell rang.

Chapter Seven

Frader.

Ben felt his hackles rise as Julie continued down the stairs toward him. She crossed in front of him, her scent spicy in his head, and he turned his head to follow her, breathe her in more deeply, before he knew what he was doing. For a moment there, just breathing in, just seeing her, not thinking, he'd have followed her anywhere.

Then she pulled open the door, and there stood Maynard Frader, Ph.D. In a bow tie.

Ben's lip curled. Julie practically stepped back into him before he realized he had to back up to let the man in the door. Begrudgingly, he took a step back.

Joe tugged at his wrist, and he leaned down to him.

"Daddy, why is Julie dressed up?"

"Because she has a date."

"What's a date?"

"I'll explain later." He straightened again and held out a hand. "Frader, hello."

Frader shook his hand, then raised an eyebrow in Julie's direction. "Shall we? Getting late, of course."

She smiled, nodded, turned to Ben. "Shall I just come over and get Marisa after I get home?"

Frader preened a bit, and the thought of him here, alone, with Julie, raised Ben's hackles again.

Inspiration struck. "I have a better idea. Why don't I stay here with both kids? I can carry a sleeping Joe home easier than you can carry a sleeping Marisa." He made his smile ingenuous.

Frader saw right through it. "Oh, I'd be happy to carry the child home for you."

Marisa shrank back against Ben's legs and threw Julie a desperate glance. Julie knew she'd been happy to spend the evening with Ben and Joe, but the thought of being carried sleeping and unawares by a stranger clearly terrified her.

Julie smiled at her, then shook her head at Frader. "Marisa feels more comfortable with people she knows. And Ben's right. I can barely carry her when she's hanging on, much less when she's fast asleep." She gave Ben a smile. "See you in a few hours, then. And thanks again."

And they were gone.

Joe tugged at Ben's wrist again. "Dad. Dad! *Dad!* What's a date?"

Ben knelt down beside him. "A date is when

grown-up men and women do something together, just the two of them, like go see a movie or go to dinner.''

''But why?''

''Why do people go on dates?'' Joe nodded. ''Well, because they like each other, and like to spend time together.''

Marisa frowned. ''Mom doesn't like *him*.''

''What makes you think she doesn't like him?''

''Because she was wearing her tights things.''

''Tights things? You mean panty hose?''

''Yep. She only wears them when she doesn't like it but she has to pretend she likes it. Like to work.''

It was an interesting point, but the image of Julie's bare legs in whisper-thin panty hose tucked under a table across from Frader, their knees brushing, didn't really do much to reassure Ben.

OKAY, SO IT WAS A DISASTER. More than a disaster, a boring humiliating disaster.

First Maynard had insisted on ordering her dinner for her—at least now she knew what Peking duck tasted like…*greasy*—and then he'd lectured her on all the things she was supposed to do with Marisa. Except none of his suggestions made any sense. Not for Marisa.

''When a child is expressing this level of anxiety, it is a parent's responsibility to show the child that her fears are ungrounded.'' He smiled tolerantly.

"Many of my colleagues would disagree with me. Wrong, of course."

He'd taken out a pipe and lit it, and they'd been asked by the manager to move to a table outside where Julie had frozen for the rest of the evening while Maynard expounded on his theories of child rearing. Ben was right. The man was a blowhard.

"While it's true that, to a child, the fear is very real, I believe that showing the child you don't think it's real is the only responsible course. To enter into the fear along with the child—which is what we do inadvertently when we allow a child's unreasonable fears to change our own behavior— simply proves to the child that the fear might be real. Must be real, in fact, because an adult is taking it seriously." He shook his head. "No, no, my experience shows that this results in fearful children retaining, rather than outgrowing, their fears."

He didn't understand. Didn't even seem to be *trying* to understand. "But Marisa does have a reason to fear being left. She's been left before."

His pipe had gone out, and he was busily relighting it, puffing to get it started again, and the smoke swirled around Julie's head. Her stomach churned with the heavy odor on top of the greasy meal. With an effort, she kept her hand at her side and didn't wave it away.

"Eh? Well, er, of course. But now that same fear is neither real nor reasonable, isn't that so? You won't leave her. Her job is to get beyond that, of course.''

Get beyond it? Up until two weeks ago, Marisa had been living it every day. ''But she's only five, and—''

''Nevertheless. Children at that age are full of baseless anxieties. They protest, they shriek, they throw tantrums. By giving in, the parent teaches the child that this is an appropriate way to deal with strong emotions.''

She gave a huff of frustration. ''Not Marisa. Marisa doesn't throw tantrums. She just weeps.''

He pursed his lips and pressed the upright index finger of his free hand against them while he thought, his gaze on a distant spot somewhere over Julie's left shoulder. ''Perhaps she needs counseling.'' He reached into his vest pocket and pulled out a business card. ''I run an anxiety group for children. We call it, Conquering Baseless Fears. Part of the discipline process, of course. Give my secretary a call and we'll see if we can't work the little girl in.''

Over Julie's dead body. Teeth clenched in what she hoped approximated a polite smile, she took the card not bothering to tell him she already had one and vowing to burn them both the minute she got home.

When he pulled up into her driveway, Julie turned to him quickly before he could shut the engine off. ''I can't thank you enough for all the advice. I had really better go see if Marisa's all right now, though.'' She held out her hand. ''Goodbye.''

He raised his eyebrows. ''Oh, quite right, of course. But do be careful about giving in to her on the anxiety issue. As I said…''

But Julie was already out of the car. ''Yes, I'm sure you're right. And I appreciate all your time. Thank you again.'' Slamming the car door, she turned and almost sprinted up the walk to her porch.

FINALLY THEY WERE BACK. When he saw Julie coming up the walk, Ben opened the door for her, his finger to his lips. He jerked his head slightly for her to follow him and led her into the living room where Marisa and Joe were curled up together on the couch, covered by an afghan, asleep. Joe had a plastic dinosaur clutched in his fist.

Julie smiled.

Ben led her into the kitchen and leaned against the counter. ''So.'' He smiled to cover his stress. ''How was the date?''

She sighed. ''Stupid. Awful. You were right, he's a pompous idiot.''

He hid his relief, or tried to. ''Then my work here is done.''

She laughed. ''He must have thought I was an idiot, too. I practically jumped out of his car before it stopped moving, I was so worried he might try to kiss me good-night.'' She wrinkled her nose. ''Pipes. Ick.''

"I beg your pardon. I myself have smoked the occasional pipe." Well, not since he was a sophomore in college, actually.

"Not before you kiss me, you don't." She blushed. "Uh, what I mean is…"

He watched her, enjoying her confusion. "I'll remember that."

She turned from him, embarrassed, and banged her head on the open corner of an overhead cabinet. "Ouch!" She rubbed her head. "Stupid cabinet, won't ever stay closed."

He reached for it, swung it once in diagnosis. "This needs to be replaced," he said, rubbing his hand over the broken hinge.

Julie laughed. "Everything in this house needs to be replaced. Or fixed. Or burned."

He shot her a glance. "Let me get my tools, I'll do it right now."

In a few minutes he was back with his tool belt strapped around his waist.

He opened his hand to show some hinges and drawer pulls he'd found in the shop. "Do you like these? I think they'd work in here."

"I love them. Are they pewter?" At his nod, she asked, "Where did you find them?"

"They're from a demolition job we did a while back, a great old house about the age of this one. They're a lot closer to the right style for this house, which is Arts and Crafts, than the ones you've got on there now." He shook his head at the hideous modern pulls that were on the cabinets. ''I don't know why they ever put these on here. They're all wrong.''

Ben grabbed a beer and carried it from cabinet to cabinet, removing hinges and knobs and replacing them with the pewter fittings. He checked each of the doors with his level, then one by one held them slightly open and let go. Each one swung slowly shut on its own.

Julie opened the cabinet over the dishwasher and let go of the door. ''Wow, this one even stays open now. I'll be able to put dishes away with both hands.'' She ran a finger over the hinge, delicate fingers tracing the curlicue of pewter. ''And these really are beautiful. But now these old cabinets look even worse, in comparison. When are you installing the new ones?'' She grinned at him.

''No, they're good cabinets. But they do need to be refinished.'' He shot her a glance. ''I'll be happy to help you with that, if you want.''

''You're a handy guy to have around.''

''Yeah, I'm a prince.'' He smiled, casually walking over to her to check the hang of one last cabinet door. As he let it swing shut, he dropped his arm to his side, brushing against her shoulder. She turned slightly, looked up at him, her eyes shining, lips curved into a smile that seemed too inviting to pass up.

He bent and kissed her, and her hand rose to his shoulder, brushed up along his neck, and he pulled her against him. For a moment, he could think of nothing but the feel of her body pressed along his.

Too soon, she broke away, placing the fingers of one hand on his lips. "Ben, the kids are in the next room." She gave her head a small shake. "I don't think it's a good thing for Marisa to see. Or Joe, for that matter. They'd get the wrong idea."

"Right." He had to do something about this whole kids thing, next time he made a move. Obviously she was enjoying this as much as he was or she wouldn't be kissing him after a date with some other guy. They had something going for them. She just needed to be free to find out what it was.

He took his arm from around her shoulders and reached for his tool belt, knocking it to the floor.

At the sound, they heard a noise from the living room.

"Mom?"

"Here I am, honey." Julie scooted past Ben into the living room. "Did you have fun with Ben and Joe?"

"Yes. But I have to go to the bathroom."

Ben stepped behind her and hefted Joe into his arms. Joe struggled a moment, then stopped moving as he drifted back off, and then they were outside and walking home.

Next time, he promised himself. Next time, he'd make sure he was alone in the house with Julie.

How he'd work that out, he had no idea. But there had to be a way.

JUST AS JULIE WAS GETTING Marisa into bed, the phone rang.

"So? How was the date? Give me all the juice." Carla, avid for news as usual.

Julie rolled her eyes as she carried the portable from her bedroom downstairs with her. "No juice. In fact, it was possibly the driest date I've ever had." She gave Carla a brief rundown of the evening.

"I told you he was a dork. But do you ever listen to me? No."

Julie laughed. "But the evening wasn't a total waste." She thought of the kiss she'd shared with Ben and smiled.

"Oh?"

"I can hear your antenna snapping to attention."

"Did you kiss Ben again?"

Julie gave her a wry smile. "How did you guess *that?*"

Carla's voice sounded smug. "You sound like a woman who's been well kissed."

Julie carried the phone and the monitor out the back door and onto the deck. "You can say that again. He can kiss, that's for sure."

"So what are you going to do about it?"

"Do about what?"

"All this kissing. You can't just keep kissing him indefinitely."

"Well, I could, I guess. But it would be frustrating. Fun but frustrating."

Carla snorted. "I'm sure it's no walk in the park for him, either."

Julie looked over at Ben's house. He was just leaving Joe's room, and she saw him snap the night-light on in the hallway. "Yeah, you're right. It isn't fair, is it? I go out with some other guy and come home and kiss Ben."

"Eh, all's fair in love and war. But unless you're falling in love with Ben, it's not very nice." Carla's voice was a bit more acerbic than usual. "I think you should date him or stop kissing him. Preferably date him."

Julie watched as a light appeared behind the blinds in Ben's bedroom. "But Marisa…"

Carla huffed. "Fine, don't date him. Stick with your dumb plan, if it'll make you feel better. But stop torturing the poor man. Not to mention yourself."

Julie swallowed. "You're right."

"Oh, my God! Call the papers! And are you actually going to take my advice, too? Just a minute, let me sit down. Okay, now you can answer."

"Yes. I'm going to take your advice. No more kissing."

The thought left Julie feeling oddly out of sorts.

MAGGIE SCANNED the Living section of the newspaper, her coffee cup on the kitchen table beside her. Anything here she could share with Ben? Usually there was something—a recipe, a review of a book on parenting. Not that he was all that receptive, but if she threw enough help up against the wall, some of it certainly ought to stick.

She skimmed the headlines. Super Spring Celebrations. No. Plant Now For Summer Color. Nothing. Local Parenting Expert To Sign Books. Aha!

She read the article. Dr. Jonathan Nearing, professor of child psychology at the University of Cincinnati would be signing his book *Helping The Anxious Child* in Dayton today, in Cincinnati on Monday.

Maggie let the paper drop. Ben wouldn't be interested, but she knew who would. Someone who had an anxious child. Someone who was looking for a parenting expert of her very own.

She smiled and looked at her watch. Saturday mornings, Ben was usually home doing yard work. If she got in the car now, she could drop in on Julie just casually, as if she'd only thought of it because she was visiting Joey. If she was lucky, she might be able to show Julie the clipping in front of Ben. He'd scoff, and Julie couldn't help but see how little faith Ben put in any expert.

If that didn't put a few questions in Julie's mind, Maggie didn't know what would. She carried her cup to the sink and grabbed her purse.

BEN WAS WIPING UP spilled milk and shoving cereal boxes back into the cupboard when there was a knock at the back door. He pushed it open to find Marisa there. "Can Joe play?"

"Sure, Marisa, come on in. Want a bowl of cereal?"

She shook her head and stepped past him. He peered out the door and saw Julie standing on her patio. "I've got her," he called. Julie nodded and turned to go back inside.

Joe looked up from his bowl. "Dad, I want to go to the park."

"Maybe later. Why don't you two play on the swings here?"

"The park swings are gooder. They swing higher."

"The park swings are *better*," Ben said. "Come on, let's go outside."

The two kids ran straight for the swing set, and Ben pushed them both for a few minutes before he heard the telephone.

"Phone!" Joe shouted, and jumped from the swing to run to the house. "I'll get it! I'll get it!" He ran inside while Ben continued to swing Marisa, waving at Julie when she peeked out the back door to check on the kids.

Joe came to the door with the phone to his ear. "Daddy," he screamed, the phone still at his mouth, "it's for you."

Ben crossed to him. "Remember, cover the

mouthpiece before you call me." He took the phone from his son, who trotted back out to the swings.

"Ben? Steiner. We've had an accident at the job site."

Ben's heart constricted. "How bad?"

"Jones'll be okay, but we need you to check something on the blueprints before we send anyone else into the area."

"Of course." Ben checked the kids—they were sitting on the swings squabbling about something— and headed into the house to get the blueprints from his office. It took him only a few minutes to find what the foreman needed, and as he was hanging up the phone, a car pulled into the driveway.

Maggie. Oh, well, Joe would be happy to see her. He stepped out the front door to meet her. "Hi, Maggie."

"Hello, Ben. I thought I'd drop by to see Joey."

"Around back, with Marisa. I ought to check on them, anyway." He started around the corner of the house.

"Oh, first let's just go give this article to Julie. I found it for her in the paper."

Great, now Maggie was running a clipping service for Julie, too. He followed her across the yard and up onto Julie's porch, where she knocked on the door.

Julie came to the door wiping her hands on a towel. She looked at Ben and Maggie in surprise. "Where are the kids?"

"Back playing on the swings. Maggie wanted to give you something."

Maggie held out a newspaper clipping. "Here, I found this for you. It's about a local child psychologist who's written a book called *Helping The Anxious Child.* I thought you might like to buy his book. And he's doing a book signing, too."

Julie smiled. "Thank you, Maggie. That's so considerate of you. Won't you come in?"

"Oh, no, I just dropped by to see Joey. I won't take up your time."

From behind them, Ben heard, "That's my daddy!"

He turned.

Walking toward them along the sidewalk, with Joe on her hip and Marisa clutching her hand, was a young girl he recognized as one of the neighbors from across the street.

"Daddy!" yelled Joe.

"Mommy!" yelled Marisa, and dropped the girl's hand. She ran to Julie. "We got lost."

Julie reached for her and pulled her close. "Lost? Where were you?"

Joe struggled, and the girl set him down. "We didn't get lost. We went to the park."

Maggie gasped. "All by yourselves?"

Joe nodded. "Well, except once we didn't know which way."

Marisa looked up at her mother. "I was scared then, because we didn't know which way was home, either." She looked at Joe, her lower lip trembling. "Joe said he knew how to go. But he didn't."

"Oh, Marisa!" Julie's voice cracked, and she held her daughter tighter. "Never, never try to go by yourself, even with Joe. Always come tell me first. Understand?" Marisa nodded.

Joe piped up. "But it was okay even though I didn't remember, 'cause somebody else's daddy showed us how to go."

"Oh my..." Maggie staggered, and Ben, his own mind reeling, reached out a hand to steady her before she fell. He helped her down onto the porch steps.

The girl stepped forward. "I saw them heading for the swings, and I didn't think they were supposed to be there alone. I asked where you were, and Joe said back home. So I brought them home."

Ben turned to Julie, and she looked at him, fear in her eyes. "Oh, Ben."

The fear in her voice nearly killed him, but he turned back to the young girl. "You're Sarah, right?" She nodded. "Thank you so much. You really took some responsibility."

From her seat on the porch steps, Maggie said, "Oh, my..."

"Thank you, thank you so..." Julie's voice cracked again. "Thank you so much. We didn't even know they were missing."

"Yeah, that's what I figured. Well, see you!"

She waved and crossed the front lawn and the street to her own house.

"Oh, my…" Maggie said, her voice shaking.

Julie looked down at her in concern. "Let me get you a glass of water." Maggie nodded weakly and Julie stepped into the house, Marisa still clinging to her.

Ben sat down beside his mother-in-law. "Maggie, I…"

She turned on him, her eyes snapping in anger. "You were supposed to be watching them?"

He nodded.

"How long had it been since you checked on them?"

He shook his head, not even trying to defend himself. "Ten minutes maybe."

"Anything could have happened to them! Anything!"

He nodded. She was right. Anything could have happened. He couldn't even stand thinking about it.

As if she'd read his mind, she said, "Well, you better think about that!"

Julie walked back through the door, a glass in her hand, her other arm around Marisa. Silent, she handed it to Maggie, who took a long sip. Julie watched Ben, her eyes wide.

"I'm sure whatever you're thinking, I deserve it." He turned to Joe. "What in the world were you thinking about? You know you aren't supposed to leave the yard."

"But we wanted to go on the swings!" Joe looked scared but defiant.

"That's it, Joe. You're not allowed out of the house for the rest of the weekend."

"Unless you say so."

Ben shook his head. "Not this weekend, I won't."

"But, Dad, you said we could go to the park later! You promised!"

In spite of his recent fear for Joe and Marisa, or maybe because of it, Joe's outrage suddenly struck Ben as funny. He covered a laugh with a cough. "And so you went by yourself? And you took Marisa with you. Nope, no park today. Go on in the house."

Joe trudged off, head down.

Ben turned to Julie. "I'm sorry."

She nodded. "I know you are."

Maggie grabbed the porch railing and struggled to her feet. "That's all? You're sorry, and that's it?"

"I don't know what else to say." He felt numb, his mind unable to process his thoughts.

"What about that you'll never let it happen again? That you'll watch your son like you're supposed to? That you won't let a four-year-old out of your sight?"

He nodded, watching Julie. "All that."

Maggie turned away from him, shaking her head.

He stepped off the porch. "Are you coming?"

Maggie eyed Julie. "I'll be over in a moment."

He nodded and looked at Julie again. "I'm really sorry."

Then he turned and crossed the yard to his own house, his thoughts tied up with what could have happened.

And because of him, almost anything could have happened. The two of them could have gotten lost. They could have tried to cross a street. They could have been abducted. And it would have been his fault.

Maybe Maggie was right, all along. Maybe Joe was better off with her.

JULIE AND MAGGIE WATCHED him go.

"Oh, my." Maggie sank back down onto the steps of the porch and took another sip of her water.

Oh, my, indeed. Julie sat down beside her, her thoughts spinning in circles inside her head. Guilt that she hadn't been watching Marisa more closely herself, anger with Ben, relief that Marisa was okay. Fear at the thought of what could have happened.

She looked behind her, into the still-open door of the house where Marisa stood silently watching her. She held out an arm, and Marisa ran into it, snuggling in close.

Julie grasped Marisa by the chin, pulled her face up to look into it. "Do you understand why what you did was a very bad thing to do?"

Marisa nodded, her eyes filling with tears. "I'm sorry," she whispered, watching Julie in fear.

Julie kissed the top of her head. "I love you, Marisa. I will always love you, no matter what. Just don't do it again." She patted her. "Go wash your face."

"And can I watch Rugrats then?"

Julie nodded, and Marisa dashed back inside the house.

"That's it? You tell her you love her and not to do it again, and that's it?" Maggie looked outraged. "You aren't even taking away TV?"

Julie sighed. "Marisa's kind of a special case."

"It doesn't matter what kind of a case she is. She needs to be punished. She needs to realize how important this is."

Julie thought of the fear in Marisa's eyes when Julie had said, "A very bad thing to do." She shook her head. "I think she'll remember. Probably too much."

Maggie pursed her mouth in disapproval. "I thought at the very least, you cared to try." She pulled herself to her feet and strode across the yard to Ben's house.

Was she right? Julie thought about it again. If Julie'd gotten angry with Marisa, Marisa would have been terrified, and not just of leaving the yard. She'd have been terrified of Julie sending her away for misbehaving.

Nope. Maggie wasn't right. Julie knew her

daughter. She was right, and she knew it. No question.

But Ben. There, Julie had some questions. She'd trusted him with her daughter. Was she wrong to have done that?

She thought of the pain on Ben's face. She knew he would always do his best for any child.

Was his best good enough?

That evening, as Julie was sitting on her deck with the child monitor and a book, Ben walked over and sat down beside her on the swing.

He reached a tentative hand out to her, then dropped it. "I am so sorry."

"I know."

"Can you forgive me?"

"I don't need to. I know you never meant anything like this to happen. The kids just got away from you." She smiled at him tenderly, and he reached a hand up to her cheek. She could see in his eyes that he was going to kiss her again.

She didn't want to turn away. Not now, not when he'd think it was because of this afternoon. But her conversation with Carla came back to her. It wasn't fair to Ben. He wasn't the man she was looking for—and a little piece of her admitted, guiltily, that the episode this afternoon had only confirmed that—and it wasn't fair to him to pretend he might be.

She turned away. She tried to do it casually, almost as if she hadn't realized he was going to kiss her.

She didn't miss the pain that tightened his face. He tried to hide it, changing the subject to talk about something he'd overheard Marisa telling Joe earlier. After a few minutes, he excused himself and recrossed the yard to his own house. Julie sat in the dark on her deck and wished life was easy at least some of the time.

MONDAY MORNING, as Julie and Marisa were leaving to get Joe, Marisa remembered her backpack and ran back upstairs to get it.

Julie called after her, ''I'm going to walk over and see if Joe's ready. We'll meet you at the car.''

''Okay.''

Progress, Julie thought with a smile.

Joe opened the door to her knock.

''Ready?''

He nodded, then turned around. ''Dad, Julie's here!'' Ben came out of the kitchen, wiping his hands on a dish towel.

''Dad, who's picking us up today?''

Ben grinned. ''I don't think anyone is picking you up. I think we'll just leave you there all night. That way Julie won't have to take you back in the morning. You'll already be there. Have you got your sleeping bag?''

Joe shrieked with delight. ''Dad! You're making a joke of it.''

"Who do you think is picking you up?"

"You are." Joe giggled.

Ben followed them out to the car as Marisa dashed out with her backpack. Julie crossed the lawn to lock the door behind her.

She heard Marisa say to Ben, "Who's picking us up today?"

"I am. I'll be there by five o'clock, during playtime."

Bless him, he always knew exactly what to say to reassure Marisa. Julie smiled, touched.

"Okay." Marisa got into the car after Joe.

Julie watched as Ben buckled the kids into their safety seats. Then, with a wave, she pulled out of the driveway.

Marisa let her go with just a few tears at Happy Learners. But was she accepting it, or was she just resigned and still fearful of what would happen if she continued to get upset every day? Was she remembering her trip to the park and thinking she had to be perfect from now on?

Whichever it was, at least Miss Barb wasn't talking about half days anymore. She did suggest Marisa might be more comfortable in all-cotton underwear.

As Julie walked into the office, Carla glanced at her and said into the mouthpiece of the phone, "Please hold." She pushed a button. "Right on cue. That's Phillipa on two."

"Does she have a camera set up in our parking

lot?'' Julie picked up the phone. "Phillipa, how are you this morning?"

"I'm the hero of the day, that's how I am. That program you wrote? Perfect. My boss thinks I'm a genius. I know it's been a hard row to hoe, but I gotta hand it to you, you really pulled my butt out of the fire with this one. I owe you one, and big time. Just wanted to let you know—you need a favor, I'm your woman." Click.

Julie looked at the phone. "I'll be damned."

"What, Phillipa on the warpath again?"

"Not at all. She was nice. Really *nice*. Maybe she met a man on that ski weekend."

"Yeah, maybe she got lucky."

Julie laughed. "You're incorrigible. Listen, I may need to be gone longer than usual at lunchtime today."

"Hot date with Mr. Right?"

"Maybe." Julie smiled. "There's a child psychologist doing a book signing at Joseph-Beth. He's written a book about anxious children. He seems to be saying all the right things to me."

"Another psychologist? I thought you'd have had your fill with that Frader guy. What about Ben?"

"What about Ben?"

"If I were you, I'd be on him like white on rice."

Julie laughed. "You were the one telling me I was being unfair to him. Besides, I just don't know.

He's a nice guy. And he really is a loving parent.
But I don't know.''

"What? What don't you know?''

She told her about the trip to the park. "It really
shook me. The kids could have been hurt.''

"Yeah, but they weren't, right? Everything
turned out fine.''

"But what if it hadn't?''

"Do you know how many nightmares parents
have about what could have happened? If everything bad that could happen to kids ever did, there
wouldn't be any kids. It's half luck, I think.''

"I guess.'' But that wasn't all of it, not really.
"Marisa's already getting so attached to him. If I
started dating him, too, and she started to see him
as a possible father—she already does, almost—and
it didn't work out, I think it would be so hard for
her.''

"But it might work out great.''

"It might.'' Julie thought for a moment. "But he
and I, we really have different ideas about parenting. He seems pretty relaxed about the whole
thing.''

"Julie, you nut! Most parents wish they could be
more relaxed, and here you are criticizing him for
it.''

Julie shook her head. "No, that isn't it. He's
good with Joe. He's even good with Marisa. Great,
really. I just don't think we're on the same wavelength when it comes to parenting, that's all. And

if he were Marisa's father, we'd need to think alike."

"Sounds like a job for Compromise Woman!" Carla held up her arms, hands fisted, as if she were a superhero.

Julie laughed but shook her head. "I don't think I should be compromising what I think is best for my kid."

At lunchtime, Julie waited in line to get her book signed. She watched as Jonathan Nearing chatted briefly with a woman in a flowered skirt while he signed her book. He gave her a charming smile as he handed it to her.

He seemed like a really nice guy. Not affected at all, like Maynard had been. He was also quite handsome. Casually dressed in khakis and a denim shirt, blond beard neatly trimmed, comfortable-looking shoes. No sign of a pipe.

When he joked with a small child standing in line with his mother, she felt her hopes rise.

Now all she had to do was find a way to extend the conversation briefly, give him the right signals.

The woman in the flowered skirt moved away from the table, and the next person in line took her place. The line inched up. Julie thought hard. A child-raising question? How to let him know she was a single mom?

She stepped into place. "Hi, I'm a brand-new mom, and I think your book is wonderful."

He smiled politely. "Well, you look marvelous for a brand-new mom. How old is your baby?"

She grinned. "Five. I just adopted her. Marisa, my daughter."

"How wonderful for you and your husband."

Julie smiled.

Chapter Eight

Julie shook her head. "Oh, no husband—I'm a single mom."

He raised an eyebrow, interested. "You adopted a five-year-old on your own? How brave of you!"

"She was in foster care, and I was her *guardian ad litem*. I just couldn't—" the memory hit Julie again and she swallowed "—just couldn't watch while she was bumped to another foster home." She smiled cheerfully.

He finished signing her book and handed it to her. "Is there any chance I could talk to you about it for a while? My next book is about the special concerns of those adopting an older child."

Julie grinned. "Only if I can pick your brain a bit."

He smiled. "You're probably more of an expert than I am at this point, but you can pick my brain all you like. I'm finished here at one o'clock— would you be able to meet me in the coffee bar here in the bookstore? I'll buy you a cup of coffee.''

Twenty minutes. Just enough time to call Carla and tell her to deal with Ed, then call Happy Learners and check on Marisa. ''I'll be there.''

Julie made her phone calls. Ed was at lunch himself with his own bosses, so probably wouldn't be back in the office for at least an hour. Marisa had had a good morning, had eaten her entire lunch and was napping.

After she hung up, Julie hit the rest room for a rapid makeup check, found a seat in the coffee bar and gave her order to the waitress just as Jonathan walked into the room. She waited while he scanned the area and waved as his eyes turned toward her booth. He smiled, a really nice smile, and stopped to speak briefly to the waitress as he crossed the room.

He held out his hand as he slid into the booth. ''Just for the sake of formality, Jonathan Nearing.''

''Julie Miles.''

The waitress set down their coffee. He smiled up at her. ''Thank you.''

Julie picked up her cup and blew on it. ''So. You're a parenting expert.''

He laughed. ''As much as one can be, when one has no children. Like I said, I'm sure you're more of an expert than I am. I think most parents are. Most just need to learn to trust themselves and their instincts.''

Julie shook her head. It was a nice thought, but she already had too much firsthand experience to the contrary. "I don't know about that. Don't you think there are an awful lot of parents out there who don't know what they're doing? Me included."

"No parent knows what she's doing. You just muddle along."

"But what if I make some hideous mistake?"

He stirred his latte, thinking. "Do you love her?"

"Do I love Marisa? Of course I do."

"No 'of course' about it. Adoption is a tricky thing, especially when you're adopting an older child. Love isn't automatic, not even for biological parents. We all have to *learn* to love our children, no matter how they come to us."

"I've known Marisa since before she was two, though."

"Two is a difficult age."

Julie made a wry face, remembering Marisa when she'd first met her. Withdrawn and fragile, apt to fall apart into tears at the least provocation, the tears often becoming so out of control it was almost frightening. But the wonderful child she'd watched Marisa develop into… She smiled, thinking about her daughter. *Her* daughter. "Yes, I love her. Very much."

He smiled at her. "I can tell, just by the expression on your face." He took a sip of his coffee. "In fact, that's one of the theories I'm working on now.

Facial expressions, and how important they are—or at least, what an important indicator they are.''

Julie's interest was piqued. ''Facial expressions?''

He nodded. ''I've been practicing for ten years, and do you know what I've noticed is a consistent difference between troubled kids who eventually come out okay and those who don't?''

She shook her head.

''It's the expressions on their parents' faces when the kids walk into the room. I watch the parents' faces, and if they light up when the kid walks into the room, I know there's a very good chance that kid's going to be okay. Even if the kid has some real problems, even if they've been doing things that are driving their parents absolutely crazy with anxiety, even if the parents have been discussing the problem in anger or in tears—when the kid walks into the room, the parents' faces change. Just a little. Just enough for me to see the parent thinks the world of that kid.''

''You mean they smile?'' She thought of Marisa and smiled herself, then laughed at his expression as he watched her.

''See? You were thinking about her, weren't you?'' He sipped his coffee. ''Sometimes their expressions just soften. Sometimes it's only brief, because most of these parents have valid reasons for being angry or worried or scared for their kids. But often it's a smile, and whatever it is, it's enough for me to see it, if I'm looking.''

"But why would that make such a difference?'' It seemed too simple—just smile at the kid, and he'll be fine.

"I have no idea.'' He laughed. "It's kind of a strange theory, definitely not ready for public consumption. But it's what I've noticed.''

Julie thought about her own mother and her weary expression. "But some kids don't get that, and they do okay anyway.''

He looked at her intently as if he knew exactly what she was talking about. "Some kids are more resilient than others.''

She looked away. "So, which came first, the smile or the okay kid?''

He sat back, laughing. "The sixty-four-thousand-dollar question. There's no way of knowing.''

"Do the kids see it? Is that why it works?'' Did she smile enough at Marisa? Julie made a mental note to smile at her as much as possible.

"I think the kids must see it. Or they must feel something else those parents are doing right.'' He leaned forward. "And I can tell you something, a lot of those parents had been doing most everything 'wrong,' if you were reading the right books.''

A picture of Ben flashed into Julie's mind, his arms wrapped around a struggling, naked Joe, his expression one of wry frustration...but underneath it, of love. "They love their kids, and it shows,'' she offered slowly, thinking. About how much Ben's love for Joe always showed on his face, in the tone of his voice when he spoke to his son, in the way he touched him. Even when Ben had completely lost his temper and spanked his son, the gesture had lacked violence. Joe had been more shocked than hurt, and he hadn't shown any signs of being frightened at all. "It shows in everything, I bet. It's just easiest to see in their faces."

He nodded. "That's all I can think."

"So as long as you don't do anything to actively screw them up, for most kids, loving them is enough to make them turn out okay?" Julie shook her head. There had to be more to it. Something she could do to make sure Marisa would be okay.

"Barring some chemical imbalance—latent schizophrenia or something like that—yeah, that's the theory. Pretty radical, huh?"

Julie thought about all the books she'd read. "You certainly don't read a lot about that in the parenting manuals."

"I have a theory about that, too." He grinned. "I have a theory about everything, did you notice?"

She laughed. "I noticed."

"How can you give instructions in how to love? They can't tell you how to feel about your child, so they focus on what they *can* tell you—how to *behave* with your child."

She stared at him a moment and then laughed in surprise. "So it's all just to sell books?"

He held a finger to his lips and looked over his shoulder in mock fear. "Shh. My publicist is around here somewhere. She might hear you." He grinned.

Before she left for work, Julie screwed up her courage and asked him if he'd like to have dinner. He agreed, and they exchanged phone numbers.

When she walked back into the office, Carla was practically bouncing off the walls in excitement. "I can't listen to you babble about some psychologist now! Ed's getting his promotion."

Julie sat down. "No kidding. Did he tell you that?"

"Get serious. Let go of information?" Carla blew air through her lips in a rude raspberry of derision. "But I heard the big guy congratulating him on his way out the door. What else would he be congratulating him about?"

"A big sale maybe?"

"Oh, perhaps one you didn't know about and didn't work on? Get real."

Julie sat back in her chair. "So. What do we do now?"

"Just sit and wait, I guess." Carla shrugged. "What else can we do?"

"We could make plans." Julie raised an eyebrow, considering it.

"Plans? What kind of plans?"

"Plans about what we're going to do if this doesn't work out the way we want it to."

The light dawned in Carla's eyes. "Oh! You mean if he hires another Account Executive in over us?"

Julie nodded.

"But what could we do about it, even if the worst did happen?"

"We could quit."

"Quit! Are you kidding? I need this job. Besides, I love this job. Except for Ed."

"We'll start our own company."

"Our own— We can't do that."

"Why not?"

"Well, we'd need..." Carla thought about it for a minute, and her expression grew bemused.

Julie smiled. "Exactly. All we need is a couple of computers and our brains. Everything else we need is right here in our heads."

"But what about clients?"

Julie raised an eyebrow. "Who does Bud Webber at Cinci Eagle call when he has a problem?"

"Me. He hates Ed."

"And Phillipa Grange practically told me I walk on water this morning."

"She hates Ed, too, ever since Ed designed that continuous loop that blew their mainframe that time."

"Exactly. If we can get recommendations from those two to take into cold calls and presentations, we ought to be able to lure enough small clients to get started with. And from there, who knows?''

Carla stared at her for a moment. ''You know, it just might work. Though I have to say, some of your plans recently haven't exactly bowled me over.'' She grinned. ''That was a segue to 'how was lunch?' As if I couldn't guess. No, don't tell me. Let's see. He sports cuff links, wears suspenders under his elbow-patched tweed jackets, you need a thesaurus to interpret him, and he leers at small children.''

Julie smiled in triumph. ''Wrong again. He's Mr. Perfect—or Dr. Perfect, I should say.''

Carla screwed up her nose. ''Really? Not even a little bit dull?''

''Not even a little. He's really nice! And he's perfect for Marisa. He wrote a *book* on anxious children and his next book is on adopting older children. He's going to be able to solve every problem we ever have before we even have it.''

Carla started humming ''Someday My Prince Will Come.''

''Stop. I know what you're saying—true love, et cetera, et cetera. Well, why can't I fall in love with this guy? It makes perfect sense. He's just what Marisa needs.''

''If you say so. I still think you should go for Ben.''

Carla was beginning to get on her nerves. ''With Ben and me it's just physical attraction. Sure, the kisses are dynamite, but it's simply one set of too-long-deprived hormones calling to another. If you think he's so perfect, you take him.''

Watching her, Carla's eyes narrowed for a moment. Then, as if coming to a decision, she said, ''Okay, maybe I will.''

Julie blinked. Carla and Ben? She sat down at her desk slowly.

''After all, he's cute, I'm adorable, what could be more perfect?''

Well, of course Carla and Ben. They were her favorite people in the world. They both made her laugh. They both could practically read her thoughts. They both approached the world with generous humor and good nature. She couldn't get along without either of them.

''Why let a great guy like that run around date-less?'' Carla said.

They'd probably be perfect together. They probably deserved each other.

She didn't think she could stand it.

''In fact,'' said Carla, still eyeing her through narrowed lids, ''why don't we double? That way there's less pressure for everyone. Just four people going out together to have a nice time. If this doc turns out as boring as he sounds, you won't have another awful date like the one with that Frader person.'' She shuddered. ''What do you think?''

The picture that came instantly to Julie's mind

was one of Carla and Ben holding hands. She shook her head. "A double date? That's so high school."

"Hey, there was a reason we did it in high school—it was fun and safe. What do you even know about this guy?"

"I'm sure Ben will hate the idea. Probably Jonathan, too."

Carla shrugged. "So try them. If they go for it, they go for it." She leaned back in her chair. "Unless, of course, you just don't want to see me with Ben."

"Okay, fine, if Jonathan doesn't care, I'll ask Ben." Since there was absolutely no chance Ben would go along with such a nutty idea, she really had nothing to worry about.

"A DATE." Ben couldn't believe his ears. Julie had another date. With another child-psychologist type.

Well, it just figured, after the thing with the park. She probably figured after that scare, Marisa needed expert attention.

He'd really blown it. No wonder she was dating other guys when it had to be painfully obvious he was nuts about her.

He laughed to mask his dismay. "You really go for these overeducated pompous types, don't you?" He'd meant it to come out teasing, but it didn't. He tried to smile to take the sting out of the words.

"He's not pompous at all."

"I'm sorry, Julie. That was out of line." He

cleared his throat. "I suppose you'll be needing a baby-sitter?"

"I will, but I wasn't going to ask you."

She didn't even trust him that much anymore. "No?"

"No. I was going to ask you to join us. You and Carla."

"You mean, a double date? Like in high school?" Ben had heard some wacky schemes before, but this one took the cake. Julie not only didn't want to date him, she wanted to bring him along on her next date. Probably to keep him away from her kid.

On the other hand, at least he'd been promoted from baby-sitter.

His first instinct was to refuse out of hand. But then he gave it some thought.

Maybe he should just go along with the craziness. At least he'd see what it was, exactly, that she thought she was looking for.

"What does Carla say about all this? Surely she realizes that if I'd wanted to ask her out, I would have."

"It was Carla's idea. I know, it's crazy. I'll just tell her you thought so, too."

Julie gave a dismissive shrug. "Besides, it's probably all moot, because we'd still need a baby-sitter. I imagine you wouldn't be too crazy about having Maggie here."

That wasn't really a problem. "No, Maggie and

I always have our differences. We never let them into her relationship with Joe. And she really likes Marisa. Maggie wants to mother every kid she sees.'' In fact, it might take the pressure off Joe to behave perfectly if Maggie had another kid to worry about for the evening.

And if he had Maggie baby-sit at his house, maybe even ask her to stay overnight...if the date with Nearing went as badly as the date with Frader, maybe Ben and Julie could drop back into Julie's house for a drink.

And Ben could take it from there. No use giving up, even when things looked pretty dark. ''Okay, I'll do it.''

The expression on her face was too perfect for words. Obviously she hadn't expected him to agree. He reached over with one hand and gently nudged her mouth shut. ''Don't act so surprised,'' he said. ''Carla's pretty cute. I didn't know she was interested.''

WHEN JULIE OPENED the door Friday evening, the sight of her almost took Ben's breath away. The light behind her shone golden highlights on her hair, and her smile was radiant. His first instinct was to touch her, and his hand moved almost on its own volition toward her face.

He stopped it with a jerk, faltering, hiding it behind a truly pathetic wave hello. She wasn't his tonight.

Not yet, anyway.

She stepped back to let him in, and her soft skirt, some flowing material, swayed with the movement, dragging his gaze irresistibly to her hips, her calves, her ankles.

He swallowed and forced himself to return his gaze to her face before she could notice.

Damn, this was going to be harder than he'd thought.

He cleared his throat, trying to think of something reasonable to say to break the awkward silence. "Uh, Marisa ready?"

She turned, her hair brushing across her neck with the movement, and called to Marisa. "Marisa? When you're finished, why don't you run upstairs and get into your jammies? Ben's ready to take you over to play with Joe and Maggie."

"I'm finished!" Ben heard the clink of a dish on the ceramic of the sink, and then Marisa ran past him and up the stairs.

The doorbell rang, and Julie opened the door to Carla. Carla gave Ben a brilliant smile. "Hi, handsome!" Julie blinked and turned away and brushed at her skirt.

And then a car was pulling up out front, so Ben said, "And here's the man of the moment."

Carla threw a glance past him to where Jonathan was getting out of his car. She gave a sniff, cynical. "Okay, you're right, he's pretty cute," she said to Julie. "Very cute, as a matter of fact. But I'll bet he's boring.'' She turned to Julie. ''I need to hit the rest room before we get going. Back in a flash.'' She trotted up the stairs.

In a moment, Ben heard Nearing's step on the porch, and then a knock. Ben felt a surge of possessiveness that surprised him. He quelled it as best he could—which wasn't well enough, given the circumstances—and said, ''I'll get that for you.''

Julie gave him a brief smile, her teeth flashing white against her tanned face and her lips, which were a fascinating shade of red. Almost as if she couldn't have picked a more perfect shade to draw his attention.

Dammit, anyway.

He turned his back on her, deliberately removing her from his sight, and pulled open the door.

''Dr. Nearing, I presume?'' Ben didn't even try for a smile.

The good doctor flashed him a surprised, questioning glance. Okay, so maybe this one wasn't as much of a self-absorbed idiot as the last one.

Which meant he probably wasn't nearly the jerk the last one had been. Which might mean trouble.

Better keep him off guard. Ben held out his hand, and the two of them shook. Nearing watched him closely, a cautious expression on his face. Good. Cautious was good. Ben turned away as Julie stepped up behind him.

''Hi, Jonathan. You've met Ben?'' Julie looked at her watch. ''Carla's upstairs, but she'll be right back down. Then we can drop Marisa off next door.''

"Oh, good, I was hoping to meet her before we left.''

Ben quelled the impulse to frown. The guy knew what he was doing. The way to a mother's heart was straight through the kid. Julie wouldn't fall for that old smarmy trick.

Julie beamed. ''Great.'' She turned and called up the stairs. ''Marisa? You ready, honey? There's someone I'd like you to meet.''

Marisa walked cautiously down the stairs in her pajamas, her glance darting to Julie, to Ben, back and forth, unsure of herself. Ben smiled reassuringly at her.

Julie took her hand. ''It's okay, honey, it's just my date, Dr. Nearing. Jonathan, this is Marisa.''

Nearing squatted down to Marisa's height, not too near her. ''I'm so pleased to meet you, Marisa.'' He extended his hand slightly toward her. Ben could see he was giving the child the opportunity to refuse to shake hands without being rude. Marisa looked at his hand, and then at his face, and slowly she reached out her hand to his. He solemnly shook it and gave her an understated smile. ''I understand you like Beanie Babies.'' She nodded and looked down. He reached into a pocket of his jacket. ''I stopped at a drive-through for a Coke on the way home from the office tonight, and look what they had.'' He opened his hand, and there on his open palm was a small stuffed frog. "I can't remember what his name is, though."

"Hopper." It was the barest whisper, but Ben heard it.

Nearing gave her a surprised, admiring look. "You know his name?"

She nodded.

"Then I think he probably belongs with you instead of me. Would you like him?"

She nodded again, her eyes on the stuffed animal.

He extended his hand, again only slightly, not quite into her space, and she looked at him briefly and then placed her hand on the frog.

Julie smiled, her gaze flashing to Ben for a moment and then back to Marisa. "What do you say, honey?"

"Thank you very much." Just a little louder than before, not quite a whisper this time.

"You're very welcome." Nearing straightened, stepping back just slightly from the little girl, and then carefully didn't look at her again. Ben could see Marisa was watching for that, watching Nearing through lashes on downcast lids as she pretended to examine her frog.

Ben had to admit it, Nearing was good. He'd respected Marisa's space, he hadn't been smarmy or obvious at all. He'd connected with her and then given her some needed privacy.

And more, Ben had gotten the strong impression that the person Nearing was trying to touch with his gift was Marisa, not Julie. He hadn't even looked at Julie, hadn't even checked her reaction. The fact that Julie was impressed—Ben could tell just how impressed she was—was just a happy side effect for Nearing.

This was bad. This was very, very bad.

Chapter Nine

Carla trotted down the stairs, stopping halfway. "Hi," she said, curious eyes on Nearing.

Julie turned to him. "My friend, Carla. We work together. Carla, this is Jonathan."

Carla stuck her hand out. "Nice to meet you. So, you have a Ph.D., huh? Exactly what does that mean?"

Julie blushed, and Ben had to bite back a laugh. But Nearing gave Carla a surprised grin and said, "Piled Higher and Deeper, as best I can remember."

Julie laughed, and Carla grinned as she shook his hand.

Ben suppressed a groan. Worse and worse. He had a sense of humor, too.

They dropped Marisa off with Maggie, who started clucking immediately about her being outside in her pajamas.

On the way out to the car, Ben heard Carla whisper to Julie as Nearing walked ahead, "Okay, so he's pretty quick on his feet. Lots of boring guys are, I'm sure.''

''One car or two?'' Nearing asked.

''One,'' Carla shot out, as if she'd anticipated the question. ''Definitely more fun that way.''

Ben had his car keys ready. He was on Carla's wavelength on this one. ''I'll drive.''

''Well,'' Julie said brightly, settling into the back seat next to Nearing. Ben could feel her presence directly behind him, feel it when she turned slightly to look at Nearing. ''Where shall we have dinner?''

After a discussion in the car debating the merits of Thai versus Italian (''I always end up stuffing myself at Thai restaurants,'' from Jonathan, and ''But that's the best place to overeat! All those veggies, and no dessert,'' from Carla), and which Thai restaurant to choose (''Keo's, it has to be Keo's. Trust me,'' from Carla and ''Trust you? I've only just met you!'' from Jonathon), they ended up at Keo's, a dumpy-looking storefront on the edge of Over-The-Rhine.''

''This is what we get for trusting you,'' Jonathan said to Carla, looking around in mock nervousness at the gritty neighborhood.

''Oh, buck up! We'll protect you,'' Carla said, laughing, and pulled open the door for him.

''I want you to know, if this goes badly, I place the blame fully on you.'' He threw back his shoulders and bravely strode into the dim restaurant.

Ben took the door just as Julie walked up and

Carla leaned into her and said, "Okay, so he isn't boring, either. I'm sure he has any number of other faults, which we shall soon discover." Carla sailed past, and Julie turned to glance at Ben, a bemused expression on her face. He didn't know what had put it there, but it made him ache once again to reach out to her, to touch her. He only just stopped himself from touching her as he followed her through the door.

In the dim interior of the restaurant, Julie had paused to get her bearings, and Ben nearly stumbled into her, catching a whiff of her elusive scent as he stopped short of touching her. She turned to him as if he had touched her, and then the waitress led them to their table.

Sitting beside Carla, Ben tried to keep his mind off the fact that Julie's feet kept brushing his whenever she crossed or uncrossed her legs. It made it hard for him to keep his mind on the conversation or even on the meal. They ordered spring rolls and hot-and-sour soup and holy basil shrimp and sweet-and-sour tofu and red curry chicken. They drank Singha beer and spicy, milky cha.

Carla and Jonathan debated the merits of cha with milk versus without ("I don't like my tea with milk," from Jonathan, and "You just aren't trying hard enough," from Carla) and then Jonathon got up to answer his pager. Ben was surprised Carla didn't razz him about it, and he turned to look at her.

Carla was sitting staring into her lap, looking as if she were about to be sick.

He leaned over. "Carla? Are you okay?"

She looked up at him, then straight at Julie and said, "I have to go to the rest room."

"Oh! Uh, me, too," Julie said, and she scooted out of the booth, her knees brushing Ben's as she slid past on the other side of the booth.

When Jonathan came back to the table, he was peering behind him into the hallway. "I just passed Carla and Julie in the hall, and I don't think either of them even saw me. What was that all about?"

"I think maybe Keo's isn't agreeing with Carla."

"Serves her right for bringing us to this dive," Jonathan said, but he shot a worried eye toward the hallway to the rest rooms.

MAGGIE READ one last bedtime story to Joe and Marisa and tucked them into bed, Marisa on Ben's bed and Joe in his own.

Since Ben had insisted she not try to drive home late, she got herself ready for bed. He could be a very thoughtful man when he tried.

She was satisfied. This Carla seemed even less mature and settled than Julie, but Maggie could tell from the way Ben spoke of the evening that he hadn't been interested in Carla. No danger there. And this would give Julie a chance to see how far short Ben fell in comparison to a real expert like Dr. Jonathan Nearing. Even if things didn't work out between Julie and Dr. Nearing, seeing them side by side ought to put Julie firmly in mind of what Ben was lacking.

And maybe Ben would see his own shortcomings, too.

Not a bad night's work. She smiled in satisfaction.

JULIE FOLLOWED CARLA into the rest room. Carla closed the door behind her, locked it and leaned against it. She paced from one end of the little room to the other and back again. Julie watched her, fighting a small smile.

Carla turned to her, tried to speak. She paced again, once, twice, up and back. She turned to Julie again, held up a hand, opened her mouth...and turned away.

Julie put her arms around her friend. "Carla, what is it? Are you okay?"

Carla looked at her through teary eyes. "I can't say it."

Julie hugged her. "Just say it."

"You'll hate me."

"I could never hate you." Julie smiled.

"You know! You already know." Carla hiccuped. "Oh, God, I'm so awful! I'm horrible! You should never trust me again."

"Carla, I'd trust you with my life."

Carla's eyes filled again. "Just not with your boyfriends." She wailed, "I am so sorry."

Julie suppressed a sigh. She'd thought that was it. "Don't be. I'm happy for you."

"I'd hate me if I were you."

"Please. You didn't set out to click with him more than I did. You're just being yourself, and you could easily have clicked with Ben. But it's just...*there.*" She smiled, totally sincere. "I'm happy for you."

THE RIDE HOME WAS a little on the quiet side. Julie couldn't tell if Jonathan and Ben had any idea what was going on, but she was far too distracted to try to make things any easier. What a situation! It boggled the mind.

If the whole thing weren't so pathetic, it would be funny. All her careful plans, all her work to find the perfect man. She'd found the perfect man, all right. The perfect man for Carla.

Julie spared her friend a sympathetic thought. Poor Carla sat hunched in the front seat, uncharacteristically silent, miserable and ecstatic all rolled up in one. That was love for you.

Ben tried a couple of times to make conversation, but Carla kept coming up with the most amazing non sequitur responses. Julie could feel him getting more and more amused. She almost laughed a couple of times herself.

At home, when they all got out of the car, Julie turned to Jonathan and held out her hand. "Good night. I had a terrific time." She smiled at Carla, standing awkwardly in the driveway, and followed Ben up the walk.

"Giving them a little privacy?" he said in a low voice as they climbed the stairs.

"You noticed, too, huh?" She gave him a rueful smile.

"I sort of figured it out after Nearing asked me for the sixth time if we shouldn't go check and see if Carla was all right." He lowered his voice to a whisper and peered back at Carla and Jonathan, who were standing awkwardly together on the sidewalk. "I think he likes her."

"Carla, too. I think she's half in love already." Julie sighed. "Well, I guess I should go take Marisa off Maggie's hands." And decide what she was going to do next. Was it even worth pursuing? Maybe Marisa would get over wanting a father. Eventually.

Ben squinted over at his house. "Actually, it looks like all three of them are asleep. Maggie's staying the night, and she likes to turn in early. I don't know about you, but I could use a drink."

She nodded. "I guess a few more minutes won't hurt."

He followed her into the kitchen and waited while she poured them each a glass of wine. They wandered into the living room with their drinks.

Julie sat down on the couch. "Well, you can say I told you so. That date was some debacle, huh?"

"Oh, I don't think Carla and Jonathan would

think so.'' He sat next to her and took a sip of his wine. ''Are you upset?''

Julie shook her head and smiled, remembering the expression on Carla's face when she'd talked about Jonathan. ''I'm happy for them.''

''But for yourself?'' As he took another sip of wine, she noticed how his hand looked holding the wineglass, his fingers wrapped around the bowl, the delicate stem barely showing. The bowl had sweated, and the droplets had transferred themselves to his fingers.

She looked away and took a sip herself. ''For myself?'' Another sip to give her time to think. ''Well, okay.'' She gave him a wry smile. ''A little disappointed. He was really perfect for Marisa.''

He shook his head. ''But for yourself?''

She looked down at her wine. ''I liked him. He's a really nice guy. But I don't think I was going to fall in love with him.''

''But you'd hoped you would?''

She laughed. ''You make it sound pretty silly. I guess it is, isn't it?''

''No, not silly. But I don't think it's as easy as you might think to plan out who you'll fall in love with.''

She looked at him, curious. ''That sounded as if it came from the voice of experience.''

He took another sip of wine. ''I guess it does come from experience. When I fell in love with Rose, it was a surprise. And it almost couldn't have come at a worse time, because I'd just finished school and started my business. She wanted kids right away, and she wanted to be home with them. Being with her meant I couldn't continue to starve for my art.'' He smiled, wry, and there was that dimple again. It showed up whenever he poked fun at himself. ''It turned out for the best, though. If we'd put off having kids, Rose wouldn't have gotten a chance to have them at all. Maggie would never have been a grandmother.''

''And you?''

''I wouldn't have Joe.'' And there was that light in his eyes again, that magic that happened whenever he thought of Joe.

''Were you upset about it, at the time?''

He shook his head. ''About like you are now, I think. I was disappointed, but I was happy to see Rose happy. And later, I was thankful that I'd gone along with what she'd wanted. I think if she hadn't had a child, she would have felt her life was wasted.''

''She must have been a great mother.'' Julie smiled a little at the wistfulness she heard in her own voice.

''She was. She was so determined that Joe wouldn't be raised like she was. Wrapped in cotton wool, never allowed to take risks. She wrote me a letter before she died, telling me she didn't want Joe raised like she was. She made me promise to let Joe do all the things she never was allowed to do.''

"Has Maggie read the letter? Maybe it would help her understand why she can't seem to get through to you."

He shook his head. "I still have it, but I've never shown it to her. Rose told her how she felt. They argued about it all the time, until Rose realized she was dying and stopped arguing about that kind of thing. But for Maggie to see it on paper, to know it occupied Rose's thoughts that strongly at the end of her life? I could never do that to Maggie." He smiled, the dimple again, and she knew exactly what he was thinking.

"Wimp." She said it for him, but she softened it with a smile, and in his answering smile she saw he understood she thought exactly the opposite. "You aren't, you know. You're deciding not to use nuclear power even though you have it." She sipped her wine, thinking. "You are letting her re-write history, though."

"Yeah, I guess. The way Maggie remembers it, she and Rose worked everything out at the end. And that's what Rose wanted, for Maggie not to feel guilty about all the criticism. But somewhere down inside she still knows. I used to mention what Rose wanted when we argued about Joe, and Maggie would look confused and unhappy. If I don't remind her of it, she forgets. So I don't mention Rose anymore.''

Julie reached for his hand, and he turned to face her, the lines of his face gentle in the soft light. She reached to him, to touch his cheek, and she brushed her hand along it. The roughness of his late-evening beard crackled like electricity along the tips of her fingers, and she suddenly found she needed to breathe deeply.

He reached for her, lightly stroking her cheek, and then leaned closer. As he leaned in, she tilted her head slightly so he could find her lips. He touched his to them, lightly at first, and then as she kissed him back he cupped his hand behind her head and deepened the kiss.

She ran a hand up his chest. She felt rather than heard his groan as a vibration from within him, and he pulled her into his arms.

His breaths were coming quicker, and the sound of them sent a charge of urgency through her. He slid his hand up along her waist, under her blouse, and stroked her breast through the lacy cloth of her brassiere, and she couldn't suppress a moan as he slipped his hand inside to caress the nipple until it stood straight and hard beneath his fingers. She felt an urgency building within her and deepened their kiss again, her tongue licking over his lips, and as he slipped her blouse over her head she tugged at his shirt, wanting it off him, wanting to see his body.

She gasped a little at the sight of him in the golden light, the fine scattered hair gleaming dark in the light from the lamp on a nearby table. The muscles in his shoulders rippled as he bent his head to kiss her breasts, pushing the cup of her bra aside to suckle her nipple. She cried out at the sudden burst of pleasure, arching herself into him, pushing her nipple into his mouth.

He pulled off her brassiere as she spread her hands over his chest, playing with the light dusting of hair over his pectoral muscles, running her fingers lightly over his nipples until he gasped and kissed her again, harder, and then her hands were at his belt.

He slipped her down on the couch, his hands running up along her bare thighs under her skirt to the lace band of her underwear. He slid his hand beneath the lace and she felt his fingers, felt them touch her, and she was moist and warm. She gasped as they brushed her curls, slipped along the edges of her lips, slid teasingly inside. She arched as she felt a sudden quick contraction.

And then they were both naked, stretched out alongside each other in the soft light, and she could see the pleasure in his eyes as he ran his hands along her, rubbing up along her thigh, along her waist, up to cup her head and pull her to him. And he leaned close, kissing her lips, her cheek, her neck, suckling her breasts once more, kissing down her belly, softly rounded, kissing the moist curls. She gasped with pleasure as his tongue parted them, parted her lips, and his tongue was hot inside her, and she almost came right there from the amazing feel of it.

"Please," she panted. "I want you inside me now!"

He stretched back up, over her body, she raised herself slightly, and with a thrust he was inside her. The sudden sweet pleasure of it almost overwhelmed her. She couldn't think, she couldn't do anything but be with him.

And then she wasn't thinking anymore, she was just feeling, and as she felt herself go over the edge, she knew he was, too.

AFTERWARD, BEN HELD JULIE in his arms as they lay on the couch, wrapped around each other, dozing. In the heat of the moment, he'd almost said, "I love you," and he wanted again to say it now. But instead he simply kissed her and held her close.

He was afraid of what she would think. Of what she would say. That it would be irrevocable, once she said she didn't love him. So he stopped himself, each time, and just held her close.

After she fell asleep, he lay watching her for a few moments. Then, reluctantly, he pulled on his clothes. He crossed to his own dark house, quietly pulled a sleeping Marisa from his bed, and carried her to her own bed.

Back downstairs, he put a hand on Julie's shoulder. She half roused, and he said in a low voice, "I've put Marisa in her room. She's fine, fast asleep." Julie nodded sleepily and drifted off again. He pulled an afghan up around her shoulders, locked the door behind him and walked home again.

Maggie was up, waiting for him in the living room.

She sat perched on a chair in his living room, fully dressed, her bag beside her. "Ben. I heard you come in earlier and realized what time it was. Where have you been?"

He closed the door behind him. "I stopped for a drink with Julie."

"That was hours ago. Did you think I wouldn't see you come home?"

"I thought you'd be asleep. I didn't want to disturb you." That much was true enough.

"Don't think I don't know what's going on. I know what's what, you know. This kind of carrying-on, and you both have small children. Unforgivable!" With that, she picked up her bag and marched out of his house.

JULIE ROUSED WITH A START, not sure why she'd awakened. Had someone knocked on the door? And why was she on the couch?

And why did she feel so great?

She smiled to herself. And then she remembered why she was feeling great. Great. Just *great*.

She stopped smiling as a pang of anxious guilt hit her, hard. What had she done? The exact thing she had told herself she wasn't going to do.

Someone pounded on the door again. "Julie? I know you're awake."

Maggie? "Just a minute." Julie stood, tripping over the afghan that had been wrapped around her bare shoulders. She pulled on her skirt and shirt and opened the door. "Maggie? What time is it?"

"Time to come to Jesus. I'm coming in." Julie had to step out of the way or be stepped on.

Julie closed the door behind her and turned to Maggie, whose face was dark with anger.

Obviously she knew. Or thought she knew.

Maggie looked pointedly at Julie's bra, which lay on the coffee table. "Have you considered, even once, what this kind of carrying-on means to a child Marisa's age?"

Julie reddened, hoping bleakly that Maggie couldn't see her in the dim light. She'd certainly picked out the bra easily enough. Julie wondered where her panties were lying in wait to embarrass her. "Maggie, I—"

"No, let me speak my piece. I thought you'd be a good person for Ben to know, because it seemed obvious to me that you cared about your child. Or at least you did your best. But this. This! Now I see. You aren't a good influence on him. He's a bad one on you."

"Maggie, I don't think this is any of your business."

"Not my business? My grandchild is involved, too. When two parents start acting like hormonal teenagers, someone has to say something."

"All right, you've had your say."

"No, I'm not finished." She stepped closer. "Julie, I understand that people have…have *needs*. But you're a parent now, and you have to put those needs aside, for the sake of your child.'' She trailed off. ''Even if Ben doesn't see that's a problem, don't you? For the sake of your child?''

The guilt hit Julie like a sledgehammer, and she collapsed on a chair. ''I do. I know Marisa has to come first.''

''Well, then act like it.'' Maggie watched her, and her face softened. She put one hand on Julie's shoulder. ''I know it's hard to do what's right. But sometimes you have to do what's hard. Do you understand? Ben's not right for Marisa, can't you see that?''

''But he could be, Maggie. Can't you see that?''

''I can see one selfish woman thinking that because she wants something, she can make it right for her child. Well, it's either right or it's not.'' She pursed her lips together, and her voice gentled. ''And this just isn't right.''

Maggie was right about Marisa needing to be first. And that it meant putting Julie's needs second. Last night had been wonderful for Julie. But it didn't change anything.

Julie nodded. ''I know what I have to do.''

''I knew you'd see it my way,'' Maggie said. ''I knew you'd have the best interests of your child at heart.'' She nodded in satisfaction and left.

Julie sat up in her bed, waiting for dawn, thinking, unable to sleep. As the sun rose, she threw on a pair of jeans and walked downstairs to make some coffee. While she was sipping it, she heard Marisa getting up, padding downstairs, and in a moment the child walked into the kitchen in her jammies, rubbing her eyes. "What's for breakfast?"

Julie fed her through a haze of uncertainty. When she'd rinsed Marisa's cereal bowl and gotten her dressed, she said, "Want to see what Joe's up to?"

Marisa nodded eagerly. "And Ben!"

Julie cringed. That was it. That was exactly it. Marisa was already way too attached to Ben.

This couldn't happen. As much as Julie might want it, being with Ben wasn't worth the risk to Marisa. Not this fast. Maybe later, when Marisa was more secure, so that if it didn't work out, Marisa wouldn't be the one who was hurt.

She led her daughter across the backyard and knocked on Ben's back door.

He pulled the door open and stood there looking at her, dressed only in a pair of faded jeans, his feet bare. Lord, but he looked good. Her body reacted that fast.

She cleared her throat. "I thought maybe the kids could play while we, ah, talked." She raised her gaze to his.

He nodded and called over his shoulder, barely turning his head, watching her. "Joe? Marisa's here to play. Why don't you kids go down in the basement?"

"But I want to swing, high and high and high! For one minute, and then I'll pump myself."

Ben looked at Julie.

She shrugged. What did it matter? They could discuss it so the kids wouldn't understand, and privacy wouldn't make it any easier. "Let's swing them. It'll keep them occupied. We can talk as best we can."

They pushed both kids on the swing set Ben had built in the backyard.

"So I assume you want to talk about..."

Julie nodded. "Mmm-hmm. I think, you know, it just isn't a good idea."

"Why?"

Julie pushed Marisa high, and the little girl squealed with delight. "Higher, Mom!"

Joe watched closely as he and Marisa crossed each other in the air. "You can't go higher than me, because it's my swings. I can only go highest."

"I can go highest, too, if my mom pushes me highest."

"No, daddies are stronger than mommies."

"Mommies push highest, though."

"Dad, I want to be highest."

Ben gave Joe a hard push, swinging him high into the air. "Why?" he repeated, watching Julie.

"It's just a bad idea. Maybe later it would be okay, but right now...she's already getting too attached." *And so am I,* thought Julie. "She's insecure right now. If it didn't work out..."

"Why wouldn't it work out? How can you predict that at this point? No one ever knows whether things will work out."

But there was a child involved, a child who

needed something special, who needed more than anything security and consistency in her life. And how to tell Ben that Julie thought they had less chance than most couples?

"Mommy! Joe's going higher!"

She pushed Marisa harder. The swing reached the high point and flipped up a little at the end, and Marisa squealed again, delighted. "Now I'm highest!"

"I said *if* it didn't, because of our different ideas about the kids..." Julie continued.

"The kids? What does this have to do with the kids?"

"Dad-*dy!*" Ben pushed Joe's swing harder, just as Joe turned his head and said, "That's not high enough!" and the swing sailed out, and Joe's fingers slipped from the plastic-coated chain. With a cry, he sailed off the end of the swing, a stomach-lurching flight that rose and then fell hard and fast.

Chapter Ten

Joe landed on his right side and, after a stunned moment, began to cry.

Ben rushed over and knelt by his son, and Julie pulled Marisa's swing to a stop.

"Daddy, it hurts!" Joe tried to sit up and screamed in pain.

Ben was pale but calm. "Sit still for a moment, buddy. Don't move. Let me see...." Ben placed gentle fingers on Joe's right arm, and Joe cried out again. "Sorry. Sorry, buddy." He looked at Julie, the pain in his own eyes matching that in his son's. "I think it's broken."

"Oh, no!"

"I'll have to take him to the emergency room."

"I'll call them to let them know we're coming." She started toward her house.

"Use my phone. Speed dial three."

Only a parent would have the emergency room on his speed dial. She changed course and barreled into Ben's kitchen, found the phone and hit star-three.

After she'd told the nurse at the emergency room they were on the way, she raced to the backyard. "We'll drive you. Marisa, get in the car, honey. I'll grab my keys." Julie rushed across the backyard to her house, grabbed her purse from the kitchen counter and ran straight through and out the front door. Ben had Joe cradled in his arms and was coming around the side of the house, Marisa trailing behind looking frightened.

Ben buckled Joe in, then wedged himself into the middle seat, helping his son cradle the arm in his lap. Julie buckled Marisa in next to him, then carefully, trying to avoid any bumps, drove to the hospital. She heard Ben in the back seat, talking low to Joe, cuddling him close to protect him from jolts, helping him support the injured arm.

The emergency room was empty, and Joe was taken into an examining room almost immediately. As Ben carried him through a set of double doors, he turned to Julie. "Would you call Maggie? She'll be upset if she finds out later I didn't call. Tell her not to worry. Tell her not to come."

Julie settled Marisa on a chair with some blocks and stepped over to the bank of phones.

"Maggie? This is Julie."

"Oh, no. What's happened? Is Joey hurt?"

"Well, Joe's going to be fine, but I'm afraid he fell off a swing."

"I told him Joey was too young for those swings! He should still be using a bucket swing. My poor, sweet baby. Is he all right?"

"Well, Ben thinks his arm is broken. We're at the emergency room at Children's now."

"Oh, sweet heaven. I'll be right there."

"Maggie, Ben said you shouldn't worry about coming back down here. Joe's fine, they'll probably just put a cast on him and that will be it."

"Don't be ridiculous. Of course, I'm coming down. I'll be there in less than an hour." Click.

Julie had opened her mouth to protest again, and now she closed it. She hung the phone back up and went to sit down with Marisa.

After a few minutes, Ben pushed through the double doors and crossed to where Julie was sitting. He took a deep breath. "It's broken. Both bones of the forearm, so they're going to have to get a resident from orthopedics down here to set it. We may be a while. I'm sorry." He paced across the floor and back again. "I can't believe I broke my son's arm."

Her heart went out to him. "Ben, I was probably pushing Marisa too high, too. We let ourselves get distracted. It could just as easily be Marisa in there right now."

"But it's not, is it? And that's what you were going to tell me, isn't it?" The pain in his voice crept into his eyes, and she shook her head, helpless.

He took a breath. "Did you call Maggie?"

"Yes, and I couldn't talk her out of coming down."

He nodded. "I was afraid she wouldn't take no for an answer." He took a deep breath. "It'll do Joe good to see her again, though. She'll spoil him, make him feel better." A nurse poked her head out of the double doors and motioned to Ben, and he trotted across the room and disappeared through them.

By the time Maggie rushed into the emergency room, there were several more children and their families waiting for attention. Julie waved her over.

"Where is he? Where is my poor child?"

"He's waiting for an orthopedist," Julie explained.

"And Ben's just letting him sit there, in pain, with nobody helping him? I'll see about that!" Maggie strode over to the counter. "I want to see my grandson immediately."

The nurse looked up at her. "What's the name, ma'am?"

"Joseph Harbison. He has a broken arm, and no one is helping him."

"Ma'am, his father's with him, and I'm sure they're doing all they can, if you'll please have a seat."

"No, I will not have a seat. I want to see him." As she smacked the flat of her hand on the countertop, Ben pushed through the doors from the examining rooms again. "Ben! Good heavens, what happened? Why aren't you with Joey?"

"Maggie, don't worry, he's fine. He's not in pain anymore. They've set his arm, and they're wrapping it right now. I just came out to let Julie know we'd be ready to leave any minute."

She set her mouth into a firm line. "I want to see him."

"They asked us to wait here. They said they could work better without us in there."

She gasped. "Well, if it was my child, I wouldn't have left him in there alone."

Ben bit his lip. Julie could see him thinking— *but he's not your child.* But he didn't say it. Julie didn't think she'd have had so much self-control at this point.

She spared a glance for Maggie, then stood in alarm as she realized the older woman's breaths were coming very fast, her chest heaving with the effort. "Maggie, here, please sit down." Placing a firm hand beneath her elbow, Julie guided her into her vacated chair, then sat beside her. "Are you having a hard time catching your breath?" Maggie nodded, unable to speak, her face frightened.

Julie threw a glance at Ben, who nodded and hurried over to the nurse at the desk. "I think my mother-in-law is starting to hyperventilate. Is there something you can do for her right away?"

The nurse looked over, then reached beneath her desk and grabbed a plastic-wrapped package, tear-ing it open and withdrawing a small sack as she came out from behind her station. She walked to Maggie and held the bag to her nose and mouth. ''Breathe into this.'' Maggie clutched it to her face and breathed, expanding and contracting the bag over and over, then more and more slowly, until finally she brought the bag down to her lap. Her breathing was still rapid, but it was under control, and the frightened look had left her eyes.

Ben sat down beside her and put his hand on her arm. ''I know it's upsetting to get here and not be able to see him yet, but I promise you, he's fine. I wouldn't have left him if he weren't.''

The double doors from the examining rooms opened, and Joe walked out, his arm encased from fingertips to just over his elbow in a lurid purple and green cast imprinted with dinosaurs. He had a sucker in his mouth and was clutching a handful of stickers. ''Grandma! I got a cast, look. It has Godzilla!'' He held out his arm for inspection.

''Oh, you poor thing. Tell me what happened.''

Joe talked around his sucker. ''Daddy was swinging me really, really high. But he didn't mean to push me off.''

She clutched him to her as she looked up at Ben. ''I've told you and told you those swings were dangerous. Now I want you to remove that swing set from your backyard.''

Joe pulled away from his grandmother, horrified. ''No! I like swinging. I told Daddy to push me higher." He turned to his father. "Daddy, just don't push me too high again when I say, then I won't fall off, huh?"

Julie winced, watching the effect that had on Ben. "Ben, he isn't blaming you." She didn't care that Maggie could hear. "He's just looking for solutions in his own Joe way." She smiled at him.

Ben squatted down next to his son, his face tight. "Don't worry, I'm not going to take down the swings. And you're right, I shouldn't have pushed you so high."

Joe hugged him. "It's okay, Daddy. I know you did it on accident."

Maggie's eyes cut into Ben, her face tight with disapproval. "So that's what happened? He asked you to push him higher, and you did?"

Ben nodded, and Julie could feel the guilt washing off him in waves. She felt pretty guilty herself. He'd been distracted, talking to her. The whole thing was easily as much her fault as his. But the idea that he'd had his mind on something else would only make Maggie even more upset, so Julie kept her mouth shut. She could apologize to Ben in private.

Maggie shook her head in disgust. "And what happens next week when he asks you to throw him off a cliff?"

Without a word, Ben hoisted Joe onto his shoulders and carried him out of the emergency room.

TUESDAY MORNING, Julie rushed into the office a little late.

Carla looked up from her desk. "Good morning."

"Great morning. Marisa's so caught up in coddling Joe she barely remembered to say goodbye to me at preschool."

"Hooray! Next thing you know, she'll be embarrassed to be seen with you."

"Then my work will be done."

Midafternoon, the phone rang. Carla picked it up. "Carla Hartshorn." She paused, then smiled. "Oh, hi." She looked at Julie, sheepish, and mouthed, "Jonathan."

Julie rolled her eyes in mock disgust as they arranged for him to pick Carla up for dinner at five. She waited until Carla hung up and said, "So. That was my date, huh?"

Carla put her head down on her desk. "I'm sorry, I'm sorry!"

Julie laughed. "Don't be. I'm glad to see it. He's a great guy."

Carla's head shot up. "He really is, isn't he? We went to Germano's last night. He speaks Italian. Well, he speaks it well enough to translate the menu for me. And I just happened to notice he tipped twenty percent."

"Gotta love a good tipper."

"Don't you just? And he called this morning, right after our first date. How many men do *that?*"

"The ones who are falling in love, I suspect."

"Don't say it. You'll jinx it."

"Oh, please. You're both so infatuated you can't see straight."

Carla giggled.

Just before five, Ed buzzed Carla. "Carla, bring in the Cincinnati Eagle file. I need you to make some changes."

"Be right in, Ed." She glanced at Julie as she gathered up the file. "If Jonathan comes—"

"I'll tell him you changed your mind. You really aren't ready for a serious relationship."

"No, tell him I'm testing him. If he wants me, he has to prove it by heroic feats of derring-do. Starting with rescuing me from Ed." She disappeared into Ed's office.

A few minutes later, the door from the street opened and Jonathan walked in. "Julie, hi." He paused. "This is a little awkward."

Julie shook her head. "Don't feel that way. I don't. Carla's my best friend, and I can understand why you'd like her. Of course, if you hurt her, I will have to face my responsibilities. Seeing as how I introduced you."

"Your responsibilities?"

Deadpan, she drew a finger across her throat.

He tugged at his collar, feigning discomfort.

She grinned, as if to say, *Just kidding. Maybe.* She glanced at the door to Ed's office and put down her work. "Carla will be out in a minute, but in the meantime, can I pick your brain again?"

He sat down across from her in the chair in front of her desk. "Of course."

She thought for a moment. "What do you think is the most important consideration for selecting a father for a child?"

An awkward pause, and Julie was mortified to realize what she'd just said. "Oh, I beg your pardon! I don't mean us...you and me...it's just something I've been thinking about lately, thinking of the future, you know. I mean, I've always thought I'd get married and then have kids, but now I've got Marisa, and it's all out of order, and now I wonder if I...oh, this sounds so stupid! Never mind! Let's talk about something else."

"No, it's all right. I think I understand what you mean. It's just that it's such a hard question." He paused for a moment, thinking. "The most important thing parents can do for their kids—after loving them—is to love each other."

"But what if they have different opinions about child raising? If one parent thinks things should be done one way, and another a totally, completely, absolutely different way...then what?"

He shrugged. "Marriage is all about compromise, and that's an important thing for kids to learn. It's good for them to see that Mom and Dad don't always agree on things, even important things. It's not agreement between the two of them that a child needs to see—it's that they can work out their differences in an atmosphere of mutual respect.'' He smiled. ''That sounded pedantic, didn't it?''

Julie shook her head, pondering. ''No, not at all. But what if one parent knows she's—or he's—right? What if the other parent thinks Oreos are a reasonable facsimile of lunch?''

He laughed. ''I think an occasional lunch of Oreos is a lot less damaging to a child than a parent who thinks she's always right—or he—'' he gave her a gentle smile ''—and who won't or can't compromise.''

For a moment all she could do was stare at him, almost blindly.

While she thought about Ben.

Ben, holding Joe before bed every night, reading to him. Ben understanding what Marisa needed to hear almost before Julie did.

Ben kissing her. Loving her. Her body reacted, her heart picking up a beat, and she caught her breath in response.

She realized Jonathan was watching her, his lips pressed together in amusement. She blushed.

The door to Ed's office opened, and Carla shot out. She gave Jonathan a dazzling smile, and he stood. ''Hi!''

''Hi!'' Carla turned pink, and Julie almost laughed. She'd never seen Carla blush before. ''I'll be ready in just a second.''

''Okay.'' As Carla shuffled her file into her rack

of current projects, Jonathan turned back to Julie. "Think about what a child really learns from the person her parent decides to spend the rest of her life with. What's a better lesson—that you should choose a decent, caring person, or that you should choose someone who knows all the answers?"

And there was no one more decent and caring than Ben. She thought of the gentleness with which he treated Maggie, even when she lashed out at him.

Jonathan smiled and turned back to Carla, his face lighting up all over again. Carla looked past him to Julie. "Want to get some dinner with us?"

Jonathan nodded, in encouragement. "Please do."

Julie shook her head. "You two go. I have some thinking to do on the way home."

As the door closed behind them, Carla was saying, "Trilby's? No one goes to Trilby's anymore. It's too crowded." Jonathan was laughing.

Julie sighed. True love.

Carla had been right. Julie'd been going about this all wrong. If she really was going to listen to the experts, she had her expert opinion: the most important thing was for parents to love each other.

And she loved Ben.

Duh. How obvious could that be? How could Julie have been so stupid?

"Ed, I'm out of here," she called, throwing a file folder into her briefcase.

He walked out of his door, making a show of looking at his watch and comparing it to the clock on the wall. "If you must, I guess you must." He turned around and walked back into his office.

Julie sighed, knowing he'd be using this against her sometime in the future.

Back home, she rushed into the house to set down her purse and briefcase. As she was about to run back out the door to go get Marisa and see Ben, there was a knock.

Ben stood there, Joe and Marisa with him. Before Julie could say anything, Ben put his hand on his son's shoulder. "Why don't you and Marisa run around back for a minute and play before dinner?"

The kids raced outside, and Julie said, "Ben, I need to talk to you—"

Ben, his face set, held out a sheet of paper to Julie.

"What is it?" She looked at him, then took it. "A subpoena...the minor child Joseph Robinson Harbison... But this is for a custody hearing."

He nodded, and the pain in his eyes struck Julie to the heart. "Maggie. She's suing—" His voice cracked, and he swallowed. "For custody of Joe."

Julie gaped at him, her mind reeling at the thought of Ben without Joe, and there was another knock on the door. On autopilot, the subpoena still in her hand, she opened it to find a man in a rumpled brown suit.

"Julie H. Miles?"

Ben looked over her shoulder as she nodded. "Now what do you want?" His voice was harsh.

"I have a delivery."

Ben jerked an angry finger at the paper in Julie's hand. "You already made your delivery."

"Not for you, pal. For her." He reached into his inside pocket, pulled out a fat envelope and held it toward Julie.

Julie took it and frowned at it. "What's this?"

"I don't know, lady, I'm just the process server. Have a good day." And with a cautious glance at Ben, he walked quickly across the lawn, got into his car and pulled away.

Julie tore open the envelope and scanned the sheets of paper. "It says I'm a witness." She swallowed, looking up at Ben. "For Maggie."

"For Maggie?" Puzzled, he took the paper from her. "Why would Maggie call my neighbor as a witness?"

Julie shook her head and wandered over to sit down on the couch, feeling numb.

Ben read over the subpoena, then started to set it down on the desk. As he did so, something caught his eye. He did a double take and picked up a sheet of paper from atop a pile. "What's..."

Julie looked over, curious. He was holding a sheet of paper torn from a notebook.

Carla's list—Daddy Candidates.

Oh, no.

Chapter Eleven

She hurried over to snatch it from him, but he held it away. "My name is on here. What is this?" He looked at her. "It says 'The World's Best Dad Candidates.' Frader, and me."

"It was just a joke of Carla's."

"A joke? What kind of a joke?"

She reddened. "Marisa was talking about wanting a father. Carla was just goofing, you know how she kids around. She was making a list…"

"A list of possible candidates. And I'm scratched off." He looked at her. "Why am I scratched off?"

She turned away. "I just thought that being neighbors, it wasn't a good idea for us to get involved. I mean, we were good as neighbors, and Marisa was so attached to you, and she really needs security and consistency in her relationships. And what if we tried it and Marisa got her hopes up and it didn't work out? And, well, that's all. But I've changed my—"

"Don't give me 'that's all.' You thought it

wouldn't work out because I wasn't a very good father, isn't that the real problem? I see there are no credentials next to my name. And as Maggie is so happy to point out, I have many failings as a father.'' He dropped the paper onto the desk. ''Some joke. In light of your status as a witness against me, I don't find it very funny.''

''Ben—'' she started, but he interrupted her.

''Do you think I'm a good father or not?''

''Of course I do!''

''But not good enough?''

''It's not that you aren't good enough! It's that Marisa needs— That is, I thought she needed...'' She trailed off.

''You thought Marisa needed someone better, is that it?''

''Not exactly better, just...'' She gave him a look pleading for understanding. ''I thought she needed someone who could make up for my mistakes. That's all it meant. But now—''

''Now it looks like Maggie figured out exactly what you meant. And agrees with you. Congratulations.''

''Ben, I never said anything to her.''

''Maybe it's what you didn't say, then.'' He gave her a bitter smile.

Julie swallowed. He was right. ''I'm sorry, Ben.''

He shook his head and walked past her to the back door. ''I better get Joe his dinner.''

The door closed behind him, and Julie tore the stupid list into shreds.

AFTER PUTTING MARISA to bed that evening Julie paused just inside the bedroom door. The hall light was on and the door open, the way Marisa liked it. The little girl lay under the sheets, her breath sounds gentle and slow as she fell asleep. Julie stepped back toward the bed, sat on the edge and reached for her daughter. She pushed Marisa's hair back from her cheek, gently so as not to wake her.

Marisa sighed and turned a little, and her hand moved. In it was the small stuffed frog Jonathan had given her. Julie smiled. She leaned over to kiss Marisa's cheek, the skin smooth and warm beneath her lips. "Good night, sweetheart."

She rose and walked down the stairs, turning off lights, locking doors. As she passed through the dark kitchen, she glanced out the window in time to see the night-light come on in Joe's room across the yard. Ben laid Joe gently on the bed, then stooped to loosen and remove the child's shoes, pull off his jeans and tuck his feet under the covers. Then, as Julie stood transfixed, he sat on the edge of Joe's bed and reached out to touch his son's cheek.

For a moment, Ben sat there still, apparently simply watching his son sleep. Then he leaned over to drop a kiss on Joe's forehead, rose and pulled the door almost shut before leaving the room.

Julie's eyes stung with the threat of tears. She didn't blame Ben one bit for being angry with her. She *had* thought he wasn't good enough for Marisa, in a way.

But she'd never thought he wasn't the best father in the world for Joe.

SATURDAY MORNING, bright and early, Marisa looked up from her Cheerios. "Mom, can I go over to Joe's?"

Julie looked down at the little girl in consternation. How could she explain that Marisa might not be welcome over at Ben's house anymore? "Uh, why don't we finish our breakfast, and we'll see what happens after that. Maybe we could do something fun today. Hey, I know—we could go to the Taste of Cincinnati. How's that sound?"

"Can Joe and Ben come, too?"

Julie tried to smile. "We'll see, honey."

After breakfast, Marisa went out to play in the sandbox. As Julie watched from the kitchen window, Joe ran over to join her. He was a rabbit this week, he'd explained to Julie a few days earlier. And rabbits liked to dig in the sand.

A moment later, Joe returned to his house, where Ben was spreading mulch, and spoke to his father excitedly.

Then he ran back to Marisa, yelling something.

Marisa jumped out of the sandbox and headed toward the house. "Mom! Joe can go, too."

Julie bit her lip and glanced over toward Ben. She stepped out onto the lawn. "Ben?" she called. He turned, then stood.

"Joe can come with us?"

"Sure, if you really said it was okay."

"And you, too?"

He gave her a bitter smile. "I don't think so."

"But you don't mind if I take him?"

He looked at her, considering. "You didn't really think I was going to take this out on him, did you?"

"No. I didn't. I just didn't know what to expect. I know you're angry with me. I wanted to apologize."

"No apology necessary. And Joe can go, anytime." He turned back to his work.

AFTER THREE HOURS of hauling the children from food booth to carnival game to bandstand and back for more food, Julie was exhausted. Who would have thought a couple of preschoolers could wear out a young, healthy adult in such a short time?

Ben would have thought, that's who. If Ben were here, he'd be sharing it with her. And making her laugh about it.

"Mom? Can we have cotton candy?" Marisa's mouth was smeared with chocolate from the Fudge Decadence she'd just finished. Her shirt was smeared with something red—either the pizza or the fruit juice, Julie guessed. Joe was even worse.

Ben was probably going to have to throw that shirt away.

"Cotton candy? How can you possibly still be hungry?"

"But I like cotton candy!"

Julie shook her head in disgust. "Okay, but how do you ask?"

"Cotton candy, please."

"Try, 'Mom, may I please have some cotton candy?'"

"Mom, please may I get cotton candy? Please."

Julie smiled, thinking that Ben would have laughed at that. "Okay, then it's time to go. You too, Joe?"

Joe nodded, but he didn't actually look all that enthusiastic at the prospect. Julie guessed he was just being a trooper.

She bought a bag of cotton candy for the two of them to share, and then they threaded their way through the steadily growing crowd toward the parking lot.

"Mom, I'm tired. Carry me!" Marisa held up her arms.

Julie bit her lip. Marisa was looking a little red in the face. "Honey, you're too heavy for me to carry. But it's only one more block."

"But I want you to."

"I wish I could carry you and Joe. And then I wish someone would carry me, carrying you."

That appealed to Marisa's sense of the absurd. "Ben could. I wish Ben was here."

"Me, too," said Joe. "He could pick us all up."

"He could run with us, I bet." Marisa laughed.

Julie was more depressed than ever. Finally they made it to the car, and she got both sticky kids strapped in, then flopped into her own seat. With a sigh, she buckled up and started the car.

Marisa fell asleep before they cleared the parking lot.

Joe threw up as soon as they hit the highway.

BEFORE CARLA AND JULIE even had a chance to say good morning to each other on Monday, the intercom box on Carla's desk beeped.

Carla rolled her eyes at Julie. Ed didn't even have to raise his voice to talk to Carla, but he insisted on using an intercom to communicate.

She hit the button. "Yes, Ed?"

"Would you and Julie please come in here? I have an announcement to make."

Julie looked over at Carla, who mouthed, "His promotion." Julie nodded in agreement, and Carla held up a fist in the sign of solidarity.

She followed Carla into Ed's office and they sat on the couch. "Yeah, boss?"

He stood, walking around his desk. "First I want to say that working with both of you has been a terrific experience. Though you have a lot to learn about the incentive business, you've come a long way in the time I've been supervising your work.''

Julie kept her eyes on him. If she looked at Carla, she'd laugh for certain.

''And so it's with mixed feelings that I announce I've been promoted. I'll be the sales manager for this area.'' He paused expectantly.

''Congratulations, Ed. I'm sure you'll love the new job.'' Julie gave him a bright smile.

''Congratulations,'' Carla echoed.

''But, of course, we need a new Account Executive for the office. We're going to hire Scottie Newsome, a bright new graduate this year from Miami, to take the job. I'm sure it'll be a lot of work, breaking in a new boss—'' he laughed at his patronizing little joke, apparently not realizing the truth of it ''—but I'm sure you'll manage.''

Julie looked at Carla. Carla nodded. Julie leaned forward. ''Actually, Ed, Carla and I have an announcement, too. We've decided to branch out on our own. We'll give you two months' notice, but we feel it's only fair to let you know we plan to go into competition with you. We're going to start out small, but you can expect to see us pitching Cincinnati Eagle as soon as we feel we're ready.''

Ed gaped. ''You're bluffing.''

Julie shook her head. ''Ed, I know you're between a rock and a hard place—I'm sure you had some pressure to hire Romie Newsome's son. But between us, don't we all know Carla and I can do this job?''

Ed smiled. Smug and patronizing. ''Of course I did consider you for the position, Julie. But now that you've changed your priorities, I really think it's best you stay where you are. Don't feel bad. Mothers of young children often don't have the time or energy to devote to professional pursuits. In another ten years or so, you can get your career right back on track.''

Julie gritted her teeth in an attempt to maintain her smile. ''Ed, even with getting used to being a mom, I've managed to keep Phillipa Grange and my other clients happy. Carla and I feel we're ready. I'm sure it won't be easy at first, but we're betting that with the recommendations we can get from some of the clients we've worked with, we'll have a chance to bid on enough programs to keep the wolf from the door. And with that promise of business, we can get a loan to tide us over until the revenues start flowing.'' She rose and extended her hand. ''But thanks for your concern.''

Ed paled under his golf-course tan. He looked from one to the other of them and shook his head. ''Fine, I call your bluff. I'll give you until after lunch to come to your senses. If you don't, you can pack up then. Think about it. Now if you'll excuse me, I have a few phone calls to make.''

Julie nodded and she and Carla left his office. In

the outer office, they stood staring at each other for a few moments. What had they done?

"Well, I don't plan to change my mind, but I guess we're still employed for now." Julie walked over to her cubby and sat down behind her desk, feeling a little numb.

"So, what's the plan, now, boss?" Carla asked.

"He thinks we're bluffing, does he?" Julie narrowed her eyes in thought. Ed was a great salesman, but he'd never be able to play this one out. He needed them too much, and somewhere inside that pointy little head of his, he knew it. "I think he's bluffing. He'd have fired us outright if he were serious. Let's wait and see what happens."

"Well, let's not wait too long. If I'm going to be homeless, I'm going to need to find a shopping cart."

Julie tried to laugh.

After lunch, Carla and Julie waited for the next shoe to drop. Surely Ed would say something to them, ask them whether they'd changed their minds.

Julie whispered, "Have you changed your mind?"

Carla shook her head. "You?"

"No. We can do this."

Carla was typing along when the light for Ed's line lit up on her phone. A moment later, she stopped typing. Her eyes darted to Julie's.

Julie said, "Carla, remember, we aren't going to do anything dishonorable..."

Carla waved her hands, shushing her. "It's Bud Webber...yada yada, how are you, how's the golf... Ed's calling to tell him there'll be a new Account Executive working the Cinci Eagle account... Webber says that's fine, as long as I'm still on it, too... Ed's hemming and hawing...okay, he's admitting I've quit...oh, Bud, you're my new best friend. Bud's hitting the roof...and Ed better know what he's doing or he can kiss Cinci Eagle goodbye."

On Julie's phone, the button for Ed's line lit up again. Carla nodded. She was hearing this call, too. She listened for a moment, then grinned at Julie. "Phillipa Grange."

She listened again. "Oh, Phillipa, you go, girl! She just loves ripping into Ed. She's telling him he better not foist a new AE on her...now she's demanding he promote you into the position...now she's telling him she's always been uneasy with Motivation, Inc., because there are so few female Account Execs..."

Another pause while Carla listened avidly. "Oh...my...God. She's telling him that she intends to call us and tell us that if we want to start our own company, she'll hear our pitch!"

The light went off on Julie's phone. A moment later, Carla's intercom buzzed.

"Carla, would you send Julie in here?"

Carla gave her an elated smile. "Go get him, Wonder Woman!"

Ed looked up as Julie poked her head around his door. "Come on in, Julie, and close the door." He stood and walked around his desk, then perched on the front of it. "I want to talk to you about this precipitous decision you're making. I know you've enjoyed working here."

Julie nodded. "I love this job, Ed."

"Then why not just stay and keep doing it?"

Julie swallowed. "Honestly?" He nodded. "Okay, then you have to be open with me, too. What commission do Account Executives earn on programs they sell?"

He coughed. "I can't really talk specifics...."

"What's the industry average?"

More comfortable, he relaxed a little. "Around fifteen percent."

"And since I know this office did sales of over three million last year..." She deliberately left the question unfinished.

He ran a hand through his hair. "But I've all but told the Newsome kid I'd give him a job."

Julie was ready for that. "What job title did you promise him?"

Ed's brow rose in thought. "Well, I didn't actually tell him any specific title. I'm sure he's expecting a commission, though."

Julie smiled. "And is there any reason he can't take Carla's job, but with a commission?"

"A commission for an Account Assistant?"

"I've always thought the entire sales team should share the commission." She leaned forward, intent on making him see. "If I were running this office, I'd split the commission with the rest of the team. And I'd promote Carla to Account Coordinator."

Ed stared at her. "But that would mean the Account Executive would get less."

"Less money per sale, sure. But with a team whose income depends partly on sales, imagine how much more effort you might get. Incentives are our business, remember?"

His gaze lost focus for a moment, and she went for the kill. "And that would translate into extra income for the Sales Manager, too, wouldn't it?"

He gave her a sharp look.

Julie smiled. Yes! A win-win situation.

Ed's face reddened and his eyes narrowed. Alarmed, Julie wiped the smile from her face.

"You know, Julie, I don't like this kind of blackmail. Forget it. You and Carla can consider yourselves free to compete with this organization, if you really think you can. Pack your stuff, you can go today. Two weeks' severance." He stood. "Oh, and please don't take any files with you. Any work you've done is company property."

Julie walked back out of his office, stunned. Carla stood just outside, anxious. Julie shook her head. "We were there. We *had* it. Then I blew it. I let him know I was happy with the deal. Stupid,

stupid, stupid. He always needs to win. Win-win doesn't do it for him.'' She met Carla's eyes. ''He fired me. You too, I think, though you might be able to change his mind on that. I'm sorry.''

Carla paled. Then she said, ''Hey, partner. You did your best.'' Then she grinned. ''Besides, this gives us a prime opportunity to eat Ed's lunch for him, once we take all his business away. And best of all, we won't have to work for Ed anymore.''

Julie almost cried. ''We're going to do this, I promise you. I promise you'll be able to pay your rent, if it kills me.''

Carla stood and put an arm around Julie's shoulder. ''Hey, none of this talk of it killing you. Whose couch would I sleep on then?''

BEN SAT BESIDE his lawyer inside the courtroom. He glanced over at Maggie. She refused to look at him. He sighed. How was he going to fix this? He knew what he wanted—to take his son home and forget about the whole thing. But he also wanted to do it in a way that wouldn't destroy his son's relationship with his grandmother.

He leaned over to Jerry. ''Remember, nothing about Rose's letter.''

Jerry shook his head. ''It's our best evidence, Ben. Evidence that your wife, whose interests Maggie is claiming to represent, agrees with your parenting decisions. But you're the boss. At least keep an open mind. If we need it, let's use it.''

If Maggie knew about the letter, it would almost kill her. But if he lost Joe, it would kill him. No "almost" about it.

He nodded reluctantly.

The bailiff stepped into the courtroom from a door to the side of the bench. "All rise for the Honorable Martina Nassmeyer."

The judge strode in, her robes flowing behind her, and sat down behind the bench. Her face was firm but kind. Ben closed his eyes, desperately willing her to understand he was doing the best he could. She looked up and nodded to the bailiff.

The bailiff stood. "The matter of *Robinson* v. *Harbison,* in the matter of the minor child Joseph Robinson Harbison."

"Are the parties present?"

Maggie's lawyer rose, Maggie standing beside her still avoiding looking at Ben. "Jennifer Dwyer, representing Margaret Robinson, Your Honor."

The judge looked over at Jerry, and he and Ben also stood. Now they were all on their feet except the judge. "Jerry Klein, representing Benjamin Harbison."

"Ms. Dwyer, would you like to make an opening statement?"

"Yes, Your Honor. Margaret Robinson is the maternal grandmother of four-year-old Joseph Harbison. She's become increasingly concerned with the health and well-being of the child and is suing for custody. The minor child would be better off with a relative caring for him full-time at home, rather than spending most of his day in an inferior day-care center. Mrs. Robinson, who is retired, is able to stay with him all day and center her life around him. Mr. Harbison works full-time, and the child spends most of his waking hours in day care.

"In addition, Mrs. Robinson believes there are neglect issues. Joey has been seen three times in just the past year in the emergency room at Children's Hospital. There are other issues as well."

The judge nodded, making notes, and Ben's heart sank. She looked at Jerry. "And you, Mr. Klein?"

"Your Honor, Mr. Harbison is a single parent, doing his level best as all single parents do, dealing with child raising alone and without help. If long hours spent in day care is a reason to declare a parent unfit in Hamilton County, then every working single parent in the county is going to have to quit working and go on welfare or end up in court. That's about one hundred thousand single parents in Hamilton County. Think of the burden on the court alone, much less the burden on the taxpayers."

"Mr. Klein, let's leave the taxpayers and the rest of the community out of this, shall we, and concentrate on what's best for this child at this time?"

Jerry nodded. "Yes, Your Honor."

"Ms. Dwyer, your first witness."

"We call Mrs. Margaret Robinson."

Ben kept his eyes on Maggie as she was sworn

in and took her seat, willing her to look at him. Surely if she saw the pain she was causing, she'd relent. But she avoided meeting his gaze.

"Mrs. Robinson, can you tell us a little of the background of this situation?"

Maggie nodded. "My daughter, Rose, died two years ago. She stayed home with Joey, and when she died, he had to go directly into day care. My heart breaks for the little guy."

"But that's not the only reason for your concern?"

"No. I understand that this is a difficult situation for Ben—" She looked over at him finally, a pleading look on her face. "Really, Ben, I do." And he knew it was true. She really did think she understood. "But I have to think about Joey. The problem isn't only the day care—though I think nine hours a day is a crime. But even beyond that, he doesn't provide enough supervision when he does take care of Joey. A four-year-old needs constant watching, and Ben just doesn't do it. I'm worried that Joey is going to get hurt again, worse than he has been before."

"You say he's been in danger before, due to parental inattention? Tell us about one of those times."

Maggie looked at the judge. "I'd stopped by for a visit, unexpectedly, and found Ben in the house. Joey was nowhere to be found. Then a neighbor girl—she's probably about twelve—walked up with

Joey on her hip. She'd found him in the park, three blocks away. He told me 'someone else's daddy took me there.' I was horrified!"

"But he wasn't hurt?"

Maggie pressed her lips together. "Not that time, no. But I was still horrified. What if the man had been a pedophile?" She shuddered. "And Ben just laughed."

Ben closed his eyes, in shock.

"He *laughed?*" Dwyer gave Ben a look of disbelief. "And this wasn't an unusual occurrence, this lack of adequate attention?"

Maggie shook her head. "No. Shortly thereafter Joey fell from a swing."

"And was he hurt that time?"

Maggie nodded. "He broke his arm."

"And where was his father?"

"He was the one swinging him." Indignant, as if Ben had himself thrown Joe from the swings. "Too high, of course. That's why Joey fell off."

"So was that the only time Joey was hurt because he wasn't being supervised closely enough?"

Maggie harrumphed. "Not at all. It happens on a regular basis."

Ben listened, his stomach roiling, as Maggie's lawyer took her through all of it. All the bruises, all the falls, all the trips to the ER, all the small and large failings, all of it pointing inexorably to his unfitness. And it was all true. Sure, Maggie made it sound worse than it was, but nothing she said was untrue.

Maybe he *was* an unfit parent. Maybe he should just let Joe live with Maggie.

No. He couldn't. He'd die without Joe. The very thought made him feel empty inside, made his arms ache to hold his son.

But was that fair to Joe? Didn't Joe deserve the best?

Didn't Joe deserve something better than what Ben could provide?

What was really best for Joe? To be with a father who loved him desperately but wasn't the best of all possible parents, or to be with a grandmother who loved him just as much and would spend all her time watching him, caring for him, keeping him safe?

But was that really the best? Was protecting children from every possible risk really what good parenting was all about?

Rose wouldn't have thought so.

He leaned over to Jerry. "I have an idea. There's another witness we might want to call."

Jerry pushed his legal pad over, and Ben jotted down the name—"Jonathan Nearing, Ph.D., Child Psychologist."

Jerry shook his head, puzzled. Ben leaned over. "I want to find out if a four-year-old kid can be oversupervised."

BEN HELD HIS BREATH as Jonathan Nearing was sworn in and took the stand the next day. This was a huge risk, bringing Jonathan in. It wasn't as if Ben had made a great first impression on the man. But he'd gotten a feeling from him, an instinct. Maybe Nearing could help.

Jerry stood. "Dr. Nearing, how much supervision does a four-year-old need?"

Jonathan shrugged. "As much as it takes to keep him out of serious trouble. All kids are different, so you can't really specify a certain level of supervision. At four, some need to be watched constantly to keep them from running into the street. Others can be left to play on their own as long as an adult is available nearby."

"Is it reasonable to expect a four-year-old not to get hurt occasionally?"

Jonathan shook his head. "They all get pretty well banged up, just in the normal course of growing up."

Ben breathed again. Maybe this would go all right. Maybe Nearing would save him.

"So several trips to the emergency room in a single year wouldn't necessarily indicate an inadequate level of supervision?"

Jonathan shrugged again. "Not necessarily. While it's stressful for everyone, the occasional trip to the emergency room is a fairly normal part of growing up in America."

Jerry walked back to the table and picked up a

notepad. "Dr. Nearing, can a four-year-old be *over*supervised?"

"Oh, sure. We used to call it overprotectiveness." Ben shot a glance at Maggie. She was biting her lip. Was she hearing Rose's voice in her mind?

"And is overprotectiveness a bad thing?"

Jonathan nodded slowly. "Not as bad as the opposite, of course…"

Ben's heart stopped as he saw where Nearing was going. He shot a glance at Maggie. She was nodding; she'd heard it, too. Her lawyer leaned over to her, asking her something. Maggie answered, bringing her hand down on the tabletop in emphasis.

Jonathan continued. "…but in general, it's not good."

Jerry pursed his lips, then walked over to Ben to whisper, "I'm not going any further on that one. He's backing off, getting into the area of underprotectiveness. I'm afraid it'll give them ammunition." Ben nodded his agreement. But he was afraid it was too late. Maggie and her lawyer had already pounced on it.

Jerry turned back to the witness stand. "Dr. Nearing, you also counsel families?"

"Yes, that's my primary practice, counseling families with young children."

"What would you say if you were counseling this family?"

"You mean, the father, child and maternal grand-mother, in this situation?"

"Yes."

"I'd wonder if the father wasn't perhaps on the low end of the protective range…and if the grand-mother wasn't on the high end. Especially given this situation."

"This situation?"

"Mrs. Robinson has lost her only child. It's natural for her to want to be very careful with her only grandchild." Ben shot another glance at Maggie. She was shaking her head, saying something to Dwyer.

"So you think she's overreacting?"

Jonathan shrugged. "I think if she cast her mind back twenty-five years or so, she'd remember how scary parenting is. That she wants to do it again is very brave of her, and confirms her love for this child. But four-year-olds do fall off swings and wander away from their parents without being no-ticed. And parents lie in bed at night promising they'll be better parents, praying that they figure out how."

Ben watched the judge. She was taking notes, but was she really listening?

Jerry raised his hands in an attitude of accep-tance, shrugging a little. "But it happens, even though we try our hardest to prevent it?"

"It does, and to a certain degree, it's a good thing."

Jerry narrowed his eyes as if in surprise. "Good? How can a four-year-old making it to the park three blocks from his home be a good thing?"

Jonathan laughed. "Well, it's not, of course. But every child has similar incidents in his childhood...or at least, he should."

"Should? How can that be? Shouldn't every parent be trying to prevent such incidents?" Jerry sounded disbelieving. Ben smiled. He was good.

"Yes, but not to the detriment of the child's development. The fact that Joe wandered away, that he trusted another adult, scary as that is for anyone who loves him, indicates some very important things about him. It indicates his father has done something very right. He has instilled a high level of self-confidence in his child, and he has taught that child to trust others."

"But what if that adult had abused him, or worse?"

"It would be a tragedy, and of course I'm not saying that Joe should be encouraged to wander off, or to trust strangers who approach him. But the fact that he did is an indication of his overall mental health. A child who has been neglected is needy, clingy, not outgoing. A child who has received too little parental supervision won't let his parent out of his sight. In many ways, the very fact that Joe wandered away, though we never want him to do so, is a compliment to his father's parenting skills. He's raised a confident child. A confident child is a bit more difficult on a parent, because these kinds of things do happen, and Mr. Harbison needs to teach Joe that it's Joe's job to stay nearby just as much as it's his job to keep Joe in sight. All without making Joe fearful.'' He smiled. ''It's a difficult balance.''

''So if a parent were to watch a child very closely, not allow the child to climb trees because he could fall, not allow him to carve jack-o'-lanterns because he could cut himself...''

Ben sat up and shot his gaze to Maggie. She was watching Jerry, blinking her eyes very fast. Her hands were clenched on the tabletop.

''The child might become overfearful.'' Jonathan sat forward, spoke directly to the judge. ''A four-year-old's job is to explore his world while keeping his parent in sight, just as much as the parent's job is to make sure the four-year-old is staying safe while still allowing the child as much independence as possible.'' The judge's expression didn't change, but she made a note.

''But isn't that giving the child enough rope to hang himself with?''

''Joe will be going to school soon, and if he hasn't learned it's his responsibility to stay in sight of responsible adults, he won't do well.''

''So what's your opinion of Mr. Harbison's reaction—to downplay his own fears when Joe wandered away, to tell Joe he had to stay in the house for the rest of the day?''

"I think it's not inappropriate. He took away the privilege of playing outside since Joe had shown he couldn't be trusted to stay in the yard. But he didn't react hysterically when Joe showed up safe and sound. I think it's an acceptable response."

"And if he had punished Joe harshly?"

"Joe might have had a hard time figuring out exactly what it was he'd done wrong, in my opinion. He might be more fearful about coming home to face his father than about leaving the yard."

"Thank you, Dr. Nearing."

The judge looked up from her notes. "Ms. Dwyer?" Ben took a deep silent breath. What would she do to pick apart Jonathan's testimony?

Dwyer rose. "Dr. Nearing, you say the occasional trip to the emergency room is not unexpected. What about three in the past year? Is that to be expected?"

Nearing gave a small smile. "It's a little more frequent than one would hope for."

She went in for the kill. "So you'd say that could be evidence of inattentiveness, even neglect?"

Nearing shrugged. "Certainly it isn't overprotectiveness. I wouldn't say it's evidence of neglect, though. Some kids can be a handful. I know of one new mother who had to call poison control three times in a single day. She wasn't neglectful, she was just overwhelmed."

Dwyer eyed him narrowly. "And the fact that Joe was injured due to parental inattentiveness so soon after he'd wandered off due to parental inattentiveness? That doesn't sound like a pattern to you?''

Nearing shrugged as if half agreeing. ''It could just be a single parent who's up against it.''

''But it could be neglect? Is that a possibility?'' Ben watched Jonathan.

Nearing nodded. ''It's a possibility.''

''Thank you, Dr. Nearing.'' Dwyer turned sharply to the judge. ''No further questions at this time, Your Honor.''

Ben watched the judge jot something on her pad, and his heart sank.

That evening at home, Ben read Joe to sleep. Literally. With Joe's head on his shoulder, he read practically every book the kid owned, just kept picking up books from the pile until Joe's eyes blinked shut and he almost slid off Ben's lap.

Then he sat holding him, unable to put him down. Unable to let him go. Finally Joe started to snore, and Ben tucked him under his covers.

But he didn't leave Joe's room, not for a very long time.

Chapter Twelve

One of the benefits of unemployment was not having to ask one's boss for a day off so one could appear in court. Julie glanced at the clock—she was due there in an hour. She put down a bowl of food for Mrs. Malloy, who sniffed cautiously at it, then stalked away looking injured.

"Fine, don't eat." How did the silly animal know Julie'd bought the cheap cat food this time to save a little money, make her savings last a little longer? "When you get hungry, it'll be here," she called after the offended cat.

The doorbell rang, and Julie smiled at Marisa, who was eating scrambled eggs at the kitchen table. "That'll be Carla." Thank goodness, Carla was right on time. If Julie didn't leave soon, she'd be late.

"Just me!" Julie heard her call from the other room.

"In here!"

Carla walked into the kitchen. "Hi, Marisa.

Ready for some fun today? I thought we'd go to the park. How's that sound?''

Marisa frowned and put down her fork. She crossed her arms in front of her chest, glowering at Julie. ''I want you to stay home with me again.''

Julie gritted her teeth. Just when Marisa seemed to be getting used to Happy Learners, Julie'd ended up at home and had taken her out of preschool. Marisa somehow had internalized the idea that she'd finally won the battle. ''Honey, you know I've got to go to court, to help Ben.''

''But why can't I go to Happy Learners?''

Julie would have laughed at the irony if she weren't ready to scream in frustration. It didn't seem fair that Julie should be feeling guilty for not sending her child to preschool. She'd spent too much time feeling guilty for sending her. ''Honey, since I'm not working right now, I can't send you there. Soon, though, as soon as I get working again. Okay?''

''No.'' Out came the lip. She frowned at Carla and sat back in her chair.

''Marisa, that's not polite. Carla's being a good friend, helping us by staying with you while I go to court. Now finish your eggs so I can put the plate into the dishwasher.''

Marisa leaned forward fast and shoved her plate away, hard. It skittered across the table and off the other side, bits of egg scattering across the floor.

''Marisa!'' Julie gaped at her in shock, not quite

believing her eyes. But it had been no accident. "I can't believe you just did that!"

Marisa's lip trembled, but she gave Julie a defiant look.

Julie bit her lip. She made her voice very gentle. "Apologize now, and help me clean this up."

"Then will you stay home?"

"No, Marisa, I told you. I can't stay home."

Marisa clamped her lips together and frowned at Julie, her eyebrows a furious line across her forehead.

"Fine. Your bedroom." Julie pointed at the doorway. "March."

Marisa pushed back her chair and ran from the room, and Julie and Carla heard her pounding up the stairs.

Carla clapped. Julie turned to her, a wry look on her face. "So glad you approve." She shook her head. "Honestly, I don't know what got into her. She's never done anything like that before. Never."

"Champagne time! Though I'd just as soon have coffee, thanks." She reached down a mug for herself.

Julie frowned, puzzled.

"Don't you get it?" Carla laughed at her. "Marisa just threw her first tantrum. I can't believe she's never thrown one before. She's really pretty good at it, for an amateur."

Sitting down suddenly, Julie stared at Carla.

"She did, didn't she?" Her eyes stung, quick as that. "She trusts me."

"And, better yet, you punished her for it. I'm so proud of you I could just bust." Leaning against the counter, Carla sipped her coffee.

Julie'd punished her—for something she'd been practically yearning for Marisa to do. "I punished her. I sent her to her room." She looked at Carla. "Was I too rough on her? Maybe she'll be afraid to ever do it again. Should I go apologize?"

Carla snorted. "Not unless you want to teach her that when *she* throws eggs, you're the one who apologizes."

Good point. "But what if she thinks I won't love her anymore?"

"Well, apparently she's realized egg throwing isn't going to make that happen, or she wouldn't have done it." Carla relented. "Go up and make sure she knows you still love her. But for heaven's sake, don't apologize." She grabbed a paper towel and wet it at the sink. "Go ahead, go. I'll clean up."

Julie climbed the stairs, wondering what she'd find. She pushed open the door to Marisa's room and found her crying on the bed. Stumbling in her haste, Julie grabbed her child to her, held her close. "Oh, honey, I'm—" She stopped herself. "I'm sorry I can't stay home with you. I wish I could, too. But you know, don't you, that it's not okay to throw your plate on the floor?"

Marisa nodded, miserable.

"And Carla's down there cleaning it up for you."

Marisa hiccuped and nodded. "I know."

"Then would you please apologize, and tell me you won't do it again?"

Leaning hard into Julie, Marisa said, "I'm sorry, and I won't do it anymore."

Julie leaned away enough to smile into Marisa's face. "I know you won't. But you'll have to tell Carla you're sorry, too, okay?"

Marisa looked up, wiping her eyes. "And you still love me, right?"

Julie thought her heart would explode with love for this child. "I still love you. I will always love you, even if you throw a hundred eggs on the floor." She pulled her in close again. "But you already knew that, didn't you?"

Marisa nodded and hugged her back.

When she got back downstairs, Julie poked her head into the kitchen. "Gotta go, or I'll be late." Before she could grab her coat, the phone rang.

Carla called, "Want me to get that?"

"No, it might be important." Julie picked up the phone.

"Julie, it's Ed. Ed Trantor," he added unnecessarily.

"Ed, I was just on my way out the door. Can I call you back tonight?"

"This will only take a minute. I need to ask you

about the program for Phillipa Grange. She's been giving Scottie a hard time, and I know you wouldn't want to leave us in the lurch.''

"Ed, I really have to go. I'm due in court in forty-five minutes.''

"I just need to know where the drafts are.''

She frowned. "In my file drawer, under Mills Industries.'' Where they always were, which Ed knew perfectly well.

"Oh, okay. And, ah…''

"Is that all?''

"Ah…also, what did you tell Bud Webber to do about the point system for their suggestion program?''

"Ed, the same as always!'' She gritted her teeth in frustration. "Half a cent a point, one-quarter the first year's value of the suggestion, a minimum of ten thousand points for any accepted suggestion. Now I really have to—''

He blurted out, "Julie, come back.''

She stole a glance at Carla, who was listening avidly to Julie's end of the conversation. She glanced again at her watch. Good grief, it was almost eight-thirty. "Ed, I told you what I wanted.''

"I know. Okay, you can have the position.''

"And Carla?''

"Carla doesn't even have a degree.'' He almost whined it.

She didn't have time for this. "Goodbye, Ed.''

"Okay, Carla too. She can have your old position."

"And sharing commissions?" Okay, maybe she had a *little* bit of time.

"The brass doesn't like it. I tried, I really did."

"Can I try?"

"What?" Ed sounded scandalized.

"If I put together a proposal, will you stay out of my way? Will you support it?" Might as well ask for the moon, too, while she was bargaining for the stars.

"It's going to be very unpopular with the other Account Executives." He was whining again.

"That's the deal, Ed. Take it or leave it. Honestly, I am going to be late for court if I don't go right now."

"Okay, you can do it. I'll...I won't stand in your way."

"Full support? You'll sign off on it?"

He sighed, defeated. "Full support."

"Ed, we'll be back tomorrow, bright and early. Tell Scottie I'm looking forward to working with him. Tell Phillipa I'll call her as soon as I get out of court. Now, I really have to go." She hung up and smiled at Carla. "The bad news is we're working for Ed again."

"Yee-haw!" screamed Carla. "You're brilliant!"

"I'm late for the door is what I am. Call Phillipa,

will you? Just in case Ed can't bring himself to do it. I'll be back as soon as I can.''

"No rush, boss." Carla winked at her, and Julie hurried out the door and down the walk to her car. Half an hour later, Julie gave her name to the bailiff standing outside the courtroom. Soon he was calling her inside to take the stand.

She was sworn in and took her seat, risking a look at Ben. He looked pale and tense, and her heart went out to him.

Maggie's lawyer approached the stand. "You're a neighbor of Mr. Harbison's?"

Julie nodded. "Yes."

"Tell me about the first time you met Mr. Harbison and his son."

"We were out in our backyard the day we moved in, and they came over." She threw a nervous glance Ben's way, and he was pressing his lips together. She could tell he was biting back nervous laughter over what she was leaving out.

"What was Joe wearing at the time?"

Julie swallowed in dismay. "Nothing."

"Nothing? He was wearing nothing at all?"

"Well, he'd been in the bathtub..."

Dwyer interrupted her. "Please just answer the question. What was the temperature outside?"

Julie bit her lip and shot Ben a helpless glance. "Maybe fifty degrees."

She saw Ben close his eyes. It did sound bad.

"So beyond the fact that he was inappropriately

wearing nothing outside, it was also a health issue?''

''He'd gotten away from Ben—''

''I beg your pardon? He'd 'gotten away'? How did he get away?''

Mortified, Julie tripped over her words trying to help the situation. All she was doing was digging it deeper. ''Ben had been on the phone, and Joe was in the bathtub, and when Ben came back into the room—''

''So once again Mr. Harbison wasn't providing adequate supervision? And this time in the bathtub? This seems to be a habit with him.''

Julie reddened, shaking her head in dismay. She couldn't even look at Ben again! Everything she said made things worse! ''No, that's not what—''

Jerry stood up. ''Objection, Your Honor. Not a question.''

''Comment withdrawn,'' Dwyer said before the judge could reprimand her. She turned to Julie. ''Does Mr. Harbison habitually provide inadequate supervision of his child?''

Julie sighed. ''I think Joe is just a difficult child to keep track of, more than anything. It's not Ben. Any parent would have a hard time.'' She couldn't look at Ben; she knew she was hurting his case.

''No further questions, Your Honor.''

Dwyer returned to her seat, and Jerry stood. ''Ms. Miles, you have a daughter of your own?''

''Yes.''

"And you occasionally ask Mr. Harbison to baby-sit her for you?"

"Yes."

"Why would you do that, if you felt he didn't provide adequate supervision for his own child?"

She gave Ben's lawyer a grateful smile. "Ben is wonderful with Marisa. I trust him completely with her."

"So you feel he's an adequate parent?"

"I think he's the best father in the world. Especially for Joe." She turned to the judge. "I'm sure he could do better on some things, but who couldn't? He tries harder than any parent I know." She looked at Ben, and her face was flushed with emotion. "I think he's the world's best dad for Joe."

"No further questions, Your Honor."

Dwyer stood up. "Permission to recross, Your Honor?" The judge nodded, and Dwyer turned to Julie. "If you were the *guardian ad litem* for this child, would you say he'd be safer with his grandmother?"

Julie thought for a moment. "If by 'safer' you mean would he be less likely to end up in the emergency room again, yes. But—"

"Thank you." Dwyer turned away, and Julie nearly screamed in frustration.

"Your Honor, can I just say one more thing?"

Judge Nassmeyer nodded.

Julie looked straight at Ben. "Yes, he'd be safer

with his grandmother. Physically, anyway. But if you mean where would he be more likely to grow up happy, I'd choose his father. Every time.'' She only hoped Ben knew how much she believed it.

The judge nodded, but she didn't appear very interested. ''Thank you, Ms. Miles. Witness is dismissed.''

And then Julie was standing outside the courtroom in the hallway, alone.

She wanted to talk to Ben, apologize for screwing up his case, for everything. But his lawyer had been leaning over him, talking earnestly, and Julie knew Ben had more important things on his mind than Julie's guilty feelings.

''So that's how it is. Don't think I didn't see how you looked at him in there! You're in love with him. That's why you changed your tune. I can't believe you fooled me. I couldn't figure out why you were lying to the judge. Now I know.''

Julie shook her head. ''I wasn't lying. But, Maggie, I think you're a good grandmother, too. One of the best. Joe is a lucky kid. I admire you so much for not turning this into something that would hurt Joe. I know you believe very sincerely that he'd be better off with you, but you never let Joe know that. He thinks his father and you are close, and that you both love him more than anything in the world. But you're wrong about Ben not being a good father. I think this custody suit is wrong, but I think everything else you've done is so right.''

Maggie looked at her, doubtful.

"I mean it, Maggie. I've seen the horrible things parents have done to their children in order to get back at each other. They've tried to make the other parent look bad, tried to make the child hate the other parent. You never stooped to that. I admire you very much for sticking to your beliefs but not letting those beliefs hurt Joe. He's lucky to have a grandmother who loves him as much as you do, and I know he'd do well living with you, if he ever had to."

Maggie started to say something, but Julie pushed ahead. "But, in the end, I think he's so much better off with Ben. He's lost his mother. What's he going to think if he loses his father? I've seen how kids' minds work, and it would appall you, the explanations they come up with for the losses in their lives. They usually blame themselves."

"That's ridiculous. It isn't Joey's fault. He's innocent."

"Exactly. But this doesn't just punish Ben. It punishes Joe." Julie watched as Maggie took that in, her face shocked. She softened her tone. "Even if it means he isn't raised the way you want him raised, did you ever have any question about Ben's motives? Did you ever think Ben wasn't doing the best job he could?"

Maggie bristled. "Of course not. Ben tries his hardest."

"Then why, Maggie?"

Maggie shook her head. "I tried to help him, but he wouldn't let me help." She looked at Julie. "Why won't he let me help?"

Julie could only shake her head. She reached out to Maggie. "Maybe the help you were offering isn't the help he really needs."

Maggie frowned. "I offer the help I think Joey needs." She looked a little less sure of herself for a moment, but then she set her face again. "I can only do what I think is right." She turned and walked away.

Julie sighed. With friends like Julie, Ben didn't need any enemies.

MAGGIE FOLLOWED HER LAWYER into the court-room after the lunch break. Surreptitiously she scanned the room. Yes, there was Julie, sitting in the back. Probably thought Maggie wouldn't notice her.

Maggie sniffed. Julie might think she knew what she was talking about, but what could she know? She was barely a mother herself. Maggie knew bet-ter. She had the experience. She tried harder. That was what was important. She would make Joey un-derstand this wasn't his fault.

But inside, a little niggling thought pricked at her. Joe without Ben. She'd never really examined that picture before. Would he understand? Would he think he'd been abandoned by his father? What would that do to him? She pushed the thought aside angrily.

The judge took her seat, and Jerry rose. "We call Ben Harbison." After Ben had been sworn in, Jerry asked, "Mr. Harbison, are you a good parent?"

"I used to think so." Ben paused, his gaze flickering to Maggie. "But I have to admit, it's hard work. Sometimes I think I'm doing great. Other times I think I have a lot of room to improve."

Maggie's mouth dropped a little. She'd never heard Ben admit that before.

"What's your relationship like with your son?"

Ben's face lit up. Anyone could see it, see the love for Joey. It was as plain as day. Maggie blinked once to clear her eyes.

"Joe is the greatest kid in the entire world. He's funny and bright and outgoing. He never met a stranger. He means the world to me. Our relationship is very strong, especially in the last two years."

Ben didn't say it, but Maggie thought it: *Especially since he has no mother.*

"And do you neglect him? Fail to provide adequate supervision?"

Ben paused. "I try to keep an eye on him when he's outside. That time he went to the park—he'd never left the yard before without permission. I was as shocked as everyone else."

"And yet you laughed about it?"

"I didn't laugh about him wandering away. I

tried not to laugh at something he said. He was shocked that, after all this, I wasn't going to take him to the park myself later, as I'd promised. His reasoning was just so Joe, it caught me off guard.''

Maggie smiled a bit, remembering Joey's outrage that day. Ben was right—Joey's reasoning was always purely his own.

''You've heard Mrs. Robinson's other concerns. Considering all these things, do you think your son would be better off with his grandmother?''

Ben turned to the judge. ''I think she'd do her best. I think she'd do a good job with him, even though I know for sure she'd be doing a lot of things exactly the opposite of the way I do them. I just wish she'd give me the same respect.'' Then he turned and looked straight at Maggie. ''Maggie, this is ridiculous. Can't we find some common ground here? Don't you think Joe would want us to?'' He tried once more, his tone gentle, his voice soft, barely reaching her. ''Don't you think Rose would?''

Maggie's stomach dropped to the floor.

Jennifer Dwyer was on her feet in an instant. ''Your Honor, please instruct the witness to address the court, not my client.''

Maggie stared back at Ben. She dropped her eyes and looked at her hands for a moment. She knew exactly what Rose would want. Suddenly she felt sick and ashamed.

Ben's lawyer said, "I'm finished with Mr. Harbison, Your Honor."

"Ms. Dwyer?"

"Yes, Your Honor." She picked up her pad, and Maggie grabbed her by the arm.

"No more," Maggie whispered. She swallowed, found her voice. "No more." Firm, that time.

"But, Maggie, this is the part where we destroy him," Jennifer whispered to her. "This is the part that's crucial to your case."

"No more. I don't want any more."

Jennifer looked at her hard for a long moment. She sighed. "Okay. You're the boss. I hope you don't regret it later, when the judge rules against you." She turned to the judge. "No questions for this witness, Your Honor." Ben shot Maggie an intent glance as he crossed the room to his own seat.

"We're through, Your Honor," said Ben's lawyer, and he sat down.

The judge closed her notepad and stood. "Then I'll take all of this information into consideration. I'll give you my decision on the fourteenth."

Afterward Maggie fled.

BEN CAUGHT UP with his mother-in-law as she hurried down the courthouse stairs. "Maggie!"

She turned.

"You stopped your lawyer."

She nodded, not meeting his eyes.

"Maggie, I have an idea. A way we can solve this. Why don't you move down here, to Cincinnati?"

"Move here? Oh, I couldn't."

"Why not? You could see Joe every day. You could take care of him after school."

"My bridge club. My friends…"

"Dayton's only forty minutes. And I'm sure Cincinnati has bridge."

"Oh, Ben, you don't want me living any closer than I already do."

"Maggie, it would be good for Joe. Why wouldn't I want that?"

She gave him a thoughtful look. "That's exactly what Julie said to me. She's got a better head on her shoulders than I thought." Glancing away for a moment, she shook her head. "Why are you doing this? You should hate me."

His heart broke a little for her. "I could never hate you. I know you just wanted what was best for Joe."

"But I went about it wrong. I should have worked harder to make sure things were really going to work out for Joey, and all I could think of was that I knew best."

He paused. "I think sometimes you do know best."

"When you said that about Rose…"

He felt a small pang of guilt. It had been worth

it, it had been necessary, but he'd hated hurting Maggie. "I'm sorry. I knew that would hurt you."

"No. Don't be sorry." She nodded. "It did hurt, because it made me remember all the fights I had with Rose, all the terrible fights over what I wouldn't let her do. Even when she was grown and had her own baby, she hated it when I coddled her. She hated it when I coddled him. Thank the good Lord, we moved past that before she died." She took a breath. "But I needed to be reminded."

He smiled at her and thought to himself that he should go home and tear up Rose's letter before Joe ever found it and showed it to Maggie.

"Maggie, will you at least think about it? Think about moving down here. Near enough that Joe can ride his bike to your house."

She pursed her lips. "Well. Perhaps when he's a bit older, he can ride his bike on the sidewalks."

Ben laughed.

JULIE'D SEEN BEN RACE from the courtroom after Maggie and decided to give them their privacy. Later that night she put Marisa to bed and walked out on her deck. She set two beers on the table, sat down and waited, determined to stay there until Ben gave in and crossed the backyard so they could talk.

Her heart soared when she heard Ben open Joe's window a few inches that evening. He'd seen her; he was planning to join her. She took a breath, determined to make him understand.

After a moment, he ambled over to her deck.

She set the monitor down beside her, made sure she could hear Marisa's even breathing through it.

First things first. She took a deep breath. "Ben, I'm so sorry about my testimony. I wanted so much to help you out, and instead—"

"Sorry? You did great. You would have saved us!"

"But the sandbox story—"

"Was what happened. What else could you say? You know I'd never want you to be dishonest."

"I know, but I kept thinking I could tell it in a way that wouldn't seem so..." She stopped, apparently stymied again.

"So neglectful?" He smiled.

She laughed. "Ben, for Joe, you're the best father in the entire world."

Ben stopped for a moment, staring at her, searching. She appeared to be completely sincere. "You really believe that?"

She nodded. "I think..." She spoke slowly, choosing her words carefully. "I think you really are the best parent in the world for Joe. He's such a great kid, how could you be anything but a good parent? He's outgoing and happy and he doesn't even know this is all going on. I told Maggie I don't think he even knows there's trouble between the two of you. Do you know how many parents would be wrecking their kid's relationship with her? But you treat her with respect and even love. I think that makes you more than an adequate parent. It makes you an exceptional person. Which can't help but make you an exceptional parent.''

He smiled, and he looked so beautiful to her that she reached out to him, cupped her hand to his cheek and kissed him.

He kissed her back, and she grew heady at the taste of him, losing track of herself, of the courthouse hall, of everything except Ben kissing her.

And then something he'd said intruded, and she pushed him away. ''What do you mean, *would* have saved us?''

He grinned and raised his glass. ''We're celebrating. Maggie's dropping the suit. She's going to move down here so she can help out. Something she said made me think I had you to thank for it. What did you say to her?''

''Nothing, really. All I did was remind her that you really did want to let her help. She knew it already, but she just wasn't thinking along those lines.'' She took a sip of her beer. ''Do you mind that she's moving down here?''

''I love it. It'll be so good for Joe. She'll be able to pick him up from preschool every day, be part of his life in a way she just couldn't before.'' He sat down and took a sip from his own bottle.

''I've been doing some thinking, too,'' she ventured. ''I've been thinking that if I was really looking for the world's best dad for Marisa, I couldn't pick a better daddy than you.'' He set down his bottle, looking at her. "But more than that…I couldn't pick a better man for myself, either. Ben, will you marry me?"

He smiled. "Miss Miles, this is all so fast." Then he leaned over and kissed her.

Epilogue

Julie hurried into the house through the pouring rain. Would summer never come? The entire backyard was a swamp. She set down her briefcase and went along the hall into the new master bedroom to change. Then she picked up the phone and dialed Maggie's number.

"I'm home, Maggie. You want to send them back over here?"

"Actually, would you mind if I just kept them? I told them I'd see if it was all right to stay overnight. I just bought them a video, and they want to watch it." Her voice turned coy. "And I thought maybe you and Ben could use a night alone about now. What do you think?"

Julie smiled and looked out across the backyard to the lights of Maggie's house, directly behind her. "I think you read my mind." She wasn't fooled, though. Maggie wanted to keep the kids because she wanted to make sure they got fed right. Julie didn't care a bit. It was tempting to let Maggie believe the kids never got anything but doughnuts at home, so Julie could have dinner alone with her husband every night.

She walked through the new kitchen Ben had designed for them from the dining room and kitchen of what had been her house. Now that the two close-set houses had been combined into one, the resulting house was about the same size as the others on the street. And one of the prettier ones, if she did say so herself. There was nothing Ben couldn't do, she thought.

She grabbed a beer from the fridge and walked across the backyard to Ben's shop. Since they'd combined their families, he'd stopped working construction and was building furniture full time, except for the time he spent on his carvings. He was starting to build a reputation there, too, and his work was eagerly taken by a gallery down in Clifton.

She opened the door quietly, hoping to catch Ben working. She wasn't disappointed, and she savored the opportunity to watch him for a few minutes. His shirt was off in the warm workshop, and he was hand-lathing a board for a beautiful four-poster bed he was working on. He sensed her presence and turned, a smile on his face.

"Quitting time." She handed him the beer.

"The kids home?"

"No, Maggie's keeping them for the night."

He smiled and set the beer down untouched.

"Oh, really? And what shall we do with ourselves?"

"I think we should celebrate."

"Celebrate? What are we celebrating? And where's your beer, if we're…" His gaze cut to hers. "Julie, where's your beer?"

She smiled. "I can't drink."

He stepped toward her, his eyes intent on her face, and she read the look on his face. She decided not to torture him anymore and nodded. "I thought maybe the world's best dad ought to get a chance to do it again."

He swept her into his arms and kissed her senseless. Which never was very hard for him to do.

Coming this March from

You first met the citizens of Cactus, Texas, in
4 Tots for 4 Texans when some matchmaking
moms decided they needed to get their
boys tied to the hitchin' post.

Now return to Cactus in

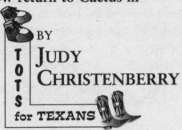

BY JUDY CHRISTENBERRY

Don't miss...

THE GREAT TEXAS WEDDING BARGAIN
March 2000
HAR #817

Megan Ford needed to get custody of her niece and
nephew—that was where good-lookin' rancher
Rick Astin came in. In exchange for some home-cooked
meals, Rick would become a daddy, and Megan would
get a whole lot more than she bargained for!

AND LOOK FOR ANOTHER ADDITION IN
SEPTEMBER 2000!

Available at your favorite retail outlet.

HARLEQUIN®
Makes any time special ™

Return to the charm of the Regency era with

GEORGETTE
HEYER,

creator of the modern Regency genre.

Enjoy six romantic collector's editions with forewords
by some of today's bestselling romance authors,

Nora Roberts, Mary Jo Putney,
Jo Beverley, Mary Balogh,
Theresa Medeiros and Kasey Michaels.

Frederica
On sale February 2000
The Nonesuch
On sale March 2000
The Convenient Marriage
On sale April 2000
Cousin Kate
On sale May 2000
The Talisman Ring
On sale June 2000
The Corinthian
On sale July 2000

Available at your favorite retail outlet.

HARLEQUIN®
Makes any time special ™

Starting December 1999,
a brand-new series about fatherhood from

HARLEQUIN®
A M E R I C A N   R O M A N C E®

THE
DADDY
CLUB

Three charming stories about dads and kids... and the women who make their families complete!

Available December 1999
FAMILY TO BE (#805)
by Linda Cajio

Available January 2000
A PREGNANCY AND A PROPOSAL (#809)
by Mindy Neff

Available February 2000
FOUR REASONS FOR FATHERHOOD (#813)
by Muriel Jensen

Available at your favorite retail outlet.

HARLEQUIN®
Makes any time special ™

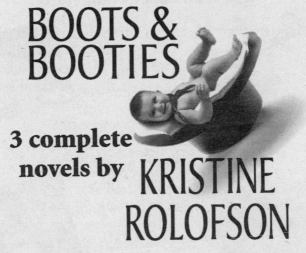

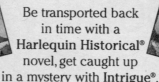